BOY BAND BABY
Bump

FERN FRASER

Editing by Violet Rae Editing services

Cover design Nichole Rose

Boy Band Baby Bump

Shelby's a fan girl on a mission to prove herself. Jameson's a bad boy seeking redemption.
Fake fling...or backstage pass to forever?

SHELBY

I've been offered the gig of a lifetime—being the tour manager for the long-awaited reunion of Soul Obsession. The woman in me is thrilled at getting to flex my organizational muscles on such a major production.

My inner teenage fan girl is squealing at being up close and personal with her favorite boy band. I never imagined I'd end up fake-dating heartthrob Jameson Munroe. Nor did I expect our staged fling could blossom into something genuine.

When a suspected stomach bug turns out to be a bun

in the oven, my orderly life plan crosses into unchartered territory.

JAMESON

This reunion tour is a love-hate endeavor. The guys and I want to play the music and thank all our fans while not having trouble and scandal follow us around. I'm keeping things strictly professional—no backstage parties, no flirty fan interactions.

My former reputation as a playboy is one hurdle that's easily solved by pretending to be in a loving, committed relationship with the orderly and buttoned-up Shelby.

Being near her grounds me in unexpected ways. When our passions get away from us, we end up with a surprise pregnancy. Now, we must navigate the media frenzy while asking ourselves the toughest question— are our feelings for each other real, or are we falling for the fantasy we created?

Chapter 1
Shelby

THE SCENT of coconut sunscreen wafts over me as I slip another sundress into my overstuffed suitcase. I let out a long breath, wiping beads of sweat from my brow with the back of my hand.

It won't be long now before I'm poolside at the resort, sipping icy cocktails. I can't wait. Although I love my job, I need a break after managing the logistics for Eclipse Entertainment Logistics' biggest event last month.

My phone rings. It's Jenna, the person covering for me while I'm on vacation. I take a deep breath. *Please let nothing be on fire.*

"I hope you're calling to tell me everything is under control," I say in a singsong voice.

"Shelby, thank God you answered!" Jenna blurts. "The roof of the venue we booked for tomorrow's show collapsed from the heavy rain. I'm hustling to secure an alternate location on the fly, but every place I call is already taken."

Poor thing. I remember experiencing the same panic my first week in this position.

"Deep breath. Walk me through what's going on," I tell her reassuringly. Keeping an even, understanding tone is crucial in stressful scenarios like this. Losing your cool never helps.

As Jenna fills me in on the details, I jot down notes, keeping my tone even. Losing your cool never helps in high-pressure situations. We methodically discuss contingency plans, even finding a tentative backup location that could work on short notice.

"Thank you, Shelby," Jenna says, sounding relieved.

Crisis averted—for now at least. After hanging up, I toss my phone aside and glance at my open suitcase. The sundresses and floppy hats call to me. But as much as I want to, I can't switch off.

I spend the next hour typing up additional instructions for Jenna. After sending the email, I return to packing. With a final shove, I zip it closed, the metal teeth coming together with a crisp rasp.

My vacation is back on track. But my relief is short-lived. My phone blares Beyonce's "Run the World (Girls)"—my boss's personalized ringtone.

I answer on the second ring, my vacation wardrobe silently judging me from within the suitcase.

"Shelby, I'm glad I caught you. I need your help with a major client," Roberto declares without wasting time.

Major clients usually mean significant financial gains, but they also come with long hours and stressful situations.

"I'm always available for Eclipse. How can I assist?"

"A major music client needs an experienced logistics manager for their upcoming stadium tour across America."

"When?" I ask, injecting enthusiasm into my voice to counteract the strain in Roberto's.

Roberto explains their current tour manager had to back out at the last minute due to a family emergency.

"I know it's out of your usual scope," my boss continues, "but I need someone I can trust, and I believe you can handle it."

Touring with a band sounds daunting, yet here I am, considering it.

"Go on," I encourage, absentmindedly pulling at the hem of the sundress I won't be wearing anytime soon. *Who needs a tan?* I silently ask myself, tossing the sunscreen back into the drawer.

"Full travel expenses, of course, with perks. VIP treatment. And the bonus is substantial. It'll make your bank account sing sweeter than a choirboy on Sunday." Roberto pauses for effect, but I'm not biting — not yet.

"How substantial?"

My boss, knowing me too well, plays his trump card. "Enough to consider a down payment on that condo you've been eyeing up," he says triumphantly.

"It's attractive, but–"

"You're perfect for this, Shelby. No strings, no distractions. You can focus solely on the job."

"Are you saying my love life — or lack of it — is a professional advantage?"

"Absolutely," he fires back without missing a beat. "No boyfriend to pine over you while you're managing the whims of pop stars."

"Flattering," I reply with a light laugh. Meanwhile, I wrack my brain, thinking about who the client could be. "Who is the client?"

"Soul Obsession. And did I mention the VIP passes for your friends?" he says almost casually.

I nearly choke on my tongue. *Soul Obsession?* The boy band my sister and her friends adored in their teens? I grew up listening to them with Ireland, watching her fawn over the members' glossy posters as she belted out their songs. When we were teenagers, she had pictures of the band members plastered all over her bedroom walls.

VIP passes.

Getting my hands on tour T-shirts for everyone–the OG's would be awesome, but VIP passes? It's next level. I love my sister, and being able to do this for her would mean everything to her and to me.

I try to keep my voice cool as I reply, "When you put it that way, how can I say no?"

Roberto whoops. "You're about to become the most envied travel manager in the industry. Your ticket and itinerary are in your inbox. The tour starts in two days. I'll have the contract sent over shortly."

I'm still reeling. The biggest boy band in the world is currently doing a reunion tour after ten years out of the spotlight.

"Um, okay," I say on a wobbly breath. "Send me the details, and I'm on it."

As soon as my boss ends the call, I hit Ireland's name in my favorites.

"Hey, sis!" Ireland answers, bubbly as always.

"Are you sitting down?"

"No, should I be? What's going on? I thought you were packing for your trip?"

"My boss called with a crazy work opportunity. I had to say yes."

Ireland gasps. "No way! What could be more important than soaking up the sun and scoping hotties by the pool?"

"My vacation is canceled because... I'm going on tour with Soul Obsession."

A piercing shriek nearly blows out my eardrum. I pull the phone away, grinning.

"Soul Obsession? Shelby, are you serious? Get me an autograph. And take pictures. Oh, my God, I'm hyperventilating!"

"How about you get those autographs yourself?" I ask, my heart pounding.

"Huh?" Ireland's confusion is clear.

"I may have VIP tickets for you and our friends," I tease.

"What? Are you kidding? This is a joke, right? Like when you told me I was descended from fairies because my big toe was smaller than my second toe."

"That was fun for a few weeks." I grin. "But I wouldn't joke about something as serious as Soul Obsession, sis. The tickets are part of the deal."

"Holy crap! Did I ever tell you that you're the best sister ever?"

I chuckle. "Yep, but it never gets old. How about you set up a call with the girls and I'll explain everything?"

"Yes! I'll message our chat group now. Shelbs, you're gonna have such a great time."

"Easy, tiger. It's just a job for me. All business," I say, though the flutter in my chest betrays me.

"Business, schmusiness! This is Soul Obsession we're talking about!"

"I'm freaking out," I admit, biting my lip. "The logistics are going to be crazy."

"You've so got this. You're the most organized person ever," Ireland insists.

A warm glow kindles inside me, pushing some of the lingering doubts into the shadows. "Thanks, sis. That means a lot."

We chat for a while longer, discussing the upcoming tour stops, and Ireland's favorite Soul Obsession songs she hopes they'll perform during the reunion tour. She was as dedicated as a fan could be before they broke up and knew all of the words to every song.

I reminisce with her about some of our great memories of their concerts and music over the years. After geeking out over the band, we finally say our goodbyes so I can start prepping.

Despite the daunting task ahead, I feel energized. Coordinating logistics for Eclipse Entertainment Logistics' largest client to date could significantly boost my career. And the bonus will put me that much closer to my dream condo.

I put away my bikinis and pack blazers, power banks, and planners. I can take my vacation later. This is too good an opportunity to pass up. And I get to share part of it with my sister and our friends.

Roberto emails the contract, and I pore over it, familiarizing myself with the tour specs. I'm confident in my skills—but intel is vital. Knowing what I'm dealing with could make the difference between smooth sailing and complete chaos.

The following two days fly by in a blur as I prepare for the trip. Ireland's friends were over the moon when I told them the news on our video chat, and have all made plans to join the tour when and where they can.

Before I know it, I'm arriving at the airport, dressed for battle in a crisp pencil skirt, blazer, and low heels. I make my way through security and find my gate. Settling into the window seat in business class, I take a deep breath and open my laptop.

I start going through the latest Soul Obsession news to ensure I'm fully up to speed before landing. Although I already know all the key details about the band, I want my knowledge to be airtight.

This high-profile assignment will test my skills, but I must prove I can handle anything. The real work will begin when we land.

Scanning entertainment sites and fan forums, I review the band's history, current status, and any drama or rumors swirling around the reunion tour.

My gaze drifts over the band lineup. The names stir hazy memories from my adolescence–Crue, Jax, Mason, Asher, and Jameson.

Jameson Munroe.

He's standing beside a private jet, wearing ripped jeans and a beaten-up leather jacket. No longer a fresh-faced teen idol, he oozes rugged bad boy appeal.

The boyish softness is gone, replaced by brooding features—hooded eyes, a Roman nose, and a square jawline darkened by stubble.

Heat rises in my cheeks as I study the contours of his face—high cheekbones, full lips curved into a seductive smirk that makes my toes curl. The man looks like sex on legs. I can't believe I never noticed him before.

I stare at a photo of him on stage, guitar slung low across his hips, his tight black t-shirt clinging to his sculpted biceps. The tattoos covering his arms only add to the edgy rock star image. A sharp pang of longing steals my breath. *Focus, Shelby.*

I continue scrolling through the news feed, but my heart sinks when I see the headline. "Jameson of Soul Obsession Caught in Scandal."

The article goes into all the sordid details about rap sensation Fuz-E Slip-R, who accuses Jameson of stealing intellectual property. According to the rapper, Jameson Munroe stole his lyrics and melodies for the solo album he plans to release after Soul Obsession's reunion tour.

The Captain announces our descent, jolting me back to reality. I slam my laptop shut, flustered. But as I smooth my hair and straighten my blouse, my heart slams against my ribs.

I expected shenanigans and attitudes—I can handle whatever they throw my way. Soul Obsession didn't hire me for my opinion. Logistics are my superpower, and I'll whip this circus into shape. I'll deliver the best tour Soul Obsession has ever had. And that's a promise.

I disembark with my game face on, ready for business. Wheeling my carry-on, I weave through the crowded terminal toward baggage claim. Before I reach the carousel, a muscular man holding a sign with "Shelby Fitzgerald" printed across the front stops me.

"That's me," I say, smiling.

"I'm Xander, Head of Security for the duration of the tour. I'm escorting you to the rehearsal studio."

Once I've gathered my bags, we head outside to where a sleek black SUV with darkened windows awaits at the curb.

The ride is quiet at first, but I soon strike up a conversation with Xander. We talk about what we need to do, when we need to do it, and how to ensure everything goes off without a hitch during the tour.

"This is it," Xander says as we pull up to our destination.

Stepping out of the vehicle, I square my shoulders and fix my gaze ahead. This is the chance of a lifetime and this is where the adventure begins.

Chapter 2
Jameson

THE STUDIO DOOR SLAMS OPEN, and our manager storms in, his face redder than Mom's overwatered tomatoes. I brace myself for the onslaught.

"Jameson!" Rick shouts, waving a tabloid in the air like it's the freaking apocalypse. "You're in hot water."

I feign nonchalance, but my stomach clenches. "What now? A fashion crime? Did I wear socks with sandals?"

"Explain this."

I snatch the tabloid from Rick, wincing at the headline —Jameson *Munroe—The Rip Off Artist—Solo Album Riddled with Stolen Melodies.*

"Plagiarism? Seriously?" I mutter, my jaw tight.

Crue shakes his head. "We're on the comeback tour of our careers, and you've got to stir up drama?"

My bandmates are all staring at me now, concern mixed with annoyance on their faces. I slump against the wall, rubbing the cross tattoo on my wrist. Fuck. I don't need this.

"It isn't true. Those songs are mine," I insist.

"Fuz-E Slip-R says you ripped off his work for your solo album," Jax pipes up. "What are we supposed to think?"

"That it's bullshit," I shoot back. "C'mon guys. You know me better than that. I worked my ass off writing new material."

Asher, our lead singer, folds his arms across his chest. "I don't know, man. Wouldn't be the first time you pulled some sketchy stuff."

I clench my jaw. I'll admit I haven't always made the best choices, but I'm not a criminal.

"The negative media could cause the label to drop us. So much for the big comeback," Rick mutters, stalking back and forth. "We gotta issue a statement denying the claims immediately."

"No way," I argue. "We stay quiet and let my legal team handle it behind the scenes."

Rick scowls but doesn't object.

We need this reunion tour to be successful, and I can't mess this up. The guys are counting on me, as much as they want to give me shit right now.

Mason finally speaks up. "It isn't a Soul Obsession album. It's Munroe's solo project. Let him sort his shit out."

I shoot our drummer, a grateful look. We may clash sometimes, but he's got my back when it counts.

"This scandal had better not tank ticket sales. I'm banking on the payoff," Jax mutters, his "rebellious" spirit rearing its head.

He was always the hothead of the band, but ten years has tempered his wild side. A little. And the money is important, but is that all this reunion means to them?

"Speak for yourself," I reply, sharper than intended. "Some of us wanted a second chance to make things right."

Crue scoffs. "Still chasing redemption, Jameson? Face it, those days are behind us. We're cashing in on nostalgia now."

Crue's words surprise me. If anyone would understand my predicament, I thought it would be him. The guy is the most empathetic of my band mates.

"The point is, we stick together," I point out.

"Jameson's right," Asher says. "We get ahead of this as a band. No infighting."

"I didn't want to take legal action, but I'll talk to my lawyer." I nod, the anger dissipating. "I care about putting on a great show for the fans. One last epic tour for the best damn supporters out there."

A murmur of assent goes through the group. Underneath the tension, we're all itching to perform and recapture the magic one more time.

"Don't screw this up," Rick warns.

I meet his gaze unflinchingly. "I won't."

I've gotten out of worse rumors unscathed—I can handle this. The music comes first, like always. This tour has to go off without a hitch. Anything else isn't an option.

Liam, our music journalist, smiles wryly. "Appearances are everything in this industry."

Jax gives me a measured look. "A girlfriend could improve your image. Make you seem more mature. Show the public you're settling down."

"Speaking from experience? I appreciate the whole fake-dating or marriage thing works for some people but that doesn't mean I want a rent-a-girlfriend service to hook me up with a woman."

I let out a harsh laugh, but instantly feel like an asshole for taking my problems out on Jax. He doesn't deserve it. I need to man up and face facts. My previous reputation as a troublemaker is the reason this is happening.

Rick's expression remains serious. "It's not a bad idea, Jameson. Showing the public you're ready to settle down will help get people on your side and repair your reputation."

I'm almost thirty-four—the party boy shtick is getting old. I'd give anything to meet a woman who wanted me—not my fame or money. But a convenient fake relationship? It'll only dig me deeper.

I frown, crossing my arms. "C'mon, man. You think any sane woman would agree to that kind of arrangement?"

Rick raises an eyebrow. "It could work for an aspiring actress or singer who'd see it as a career boost. And the paycheck we could offer wouldn't hurt."

I shake my head. "She'd get paid twice. Once by me, and again by the tabloids when she sells me out."

"Think about your acting prospects," Rick presses. "We need to rebrand you."

"Rebrand me?" I snort. "I'm not a freaking protein bar."

"The right girl could give you stability," Rick says gently.

"I'll consider it," I concede, meeting Rick's gaze. "But only if the woman is willing and understands what she's getting into."

"Sure," Rick says, a hint of relief in his eyes.

The Soul Obsession reunion tour is my main focus. I've got to make the most of the opportunity.

I pick up my guitar and strum a few idle chords. I had my first actual audition for a gritty indie film. It's not a big one, but when I pictured walking the red carpet at the premiere, there was no one with me.

How would it feel to share my life? I shake my head firmly. *Don't venture down that path*, I caution myself.

"From the top," the producer calls from the recording booth.

The opening chords of our biggest hit wash over me, the familiar melody instantly transporting me back a decade. I sway and snap my fingers to the beat, the lyrics on the tip of my tongue.

I open my eyes and see the other guys are into it, too. Jax's head bobs. Mason is rocking out, drumming a beat on his thighs. Crue's eyes are closed, and he's belting the lyrics with as much passion as ever.

Man, I've missed this feeling—the pure joy of losing myself in the music. No matter how much chaos is swirling around us, everything fades away when we're performing together.

The lyrics are imprinted on my brain after singing them hundreds of times during the height of our fame.

But the nostalgia only makes me appreciate them more now.

I'm not going to lie; some of our old songs make me cringe. We were just kids back then. But this one? It's a true classic. I'll never get tired of it.

We might have our issues, but damn if we don't still have chemistry when we hit the stage. A decade apart didn't change that. As the chorus hits, our voices blend perfectly, like old times.

I slide over to Asher, nudging him with my shoulder. He grins and nods, knowing precisely what I mean. This one's special. The song builds to its epic climax, and we all feel it. I belt out the final chorus with everything I've got.

The guys join me in the layered harmonies, our voices soaring. Damn, it feels good to perform together. We still have fire and passion for the music. As long as we have that, this reunion tour will be epic.

When the final note fades out, we stand there panting and smiling. I laugh, adrenaline and endorphins flooding my system. I live for this rush.

"Just like old times," Crue says, shaking his head in awe.

"We still got it!" Jax crows.

The rehearsal room door swings open, and Xander, our head of security, strides in, followed closely by a woman I don't recognize. But it's the self-assured way she carries herself that catches my interest. No hesitation at the threshold, no moment of star-struck awe I'm used to seeing in newcomers here.

Xander offers the woman a seat, but she stands with her back against the wall. She's wrapped up in a no-nonsense pencil skirt and blouse, dark blonde hair cinched into a tight ponytail. Her lips are pressed in a firm line, her posture rigid as her gaze sweeps over the room.

She observes us with a detached air like she's cataloging every detail. Not a crazed fan who snuck past security. When her blue eyes flick my way, I flash my most charming smile, but she pointedly avoids meeting my eyes. Her expression remains impassive. I can't get a read on what she's thinking at all.

Despite the interruption, we keep working through our setlist. I add a little extra flair when soloing, unable to resist showing off with a beautiful woman watching. But if she's impressed, it doesn't show.

When the song's final chords ring out, I let out a deep breath, rolling my shoulders to release some tension.

"That's a wrap for today, gentlemen," Rick calls, glancing up from his phone. "Guys, meet Shelby Fitzgerald, Eclipse Entertainment's best logistics manager. Please give our new team member a warm welcome."

As each guy shakes Shelby's hand, she gives them the same polite, distant smile.

I give her a mischievous grin. "Jameson Munroe. Welcome aboard, Shelby."

Shelby's grip is firm, but she doesn't linger. "Thank you. I'm looking forward to working with you all."

I'd like to see her tightly pulled blonde hair tumble free and trace the column of her neck to see if those serious blue eyes flare with something wilder.

"We're pumped about this tour. Think you can keep up with us?"

Shelby meets my gaze coolly. "I know you've been through a lot with the last-minute change, but I'll make the transition as smooth as possible. You guys can focus on the music and entertaining the fans. I'll handle everything else."

The guys exchange looks. Shelby doesn't seem easily charmed. Or intimidated. She confers with Rick in hushed tones.

I linger a moment, hoping she'll look up. But she focuses on her notes, effectively dismissing me. Message received, loud and clear.

"Yo, we still hitting up O'Malley's tonight?" Mason asks as we pack our gear.

"You know it," Crue confirms. "First round's on you for showing up late today."

Mason laughs and flips him off good-naturedly. O'Malley's—our old standby. It's been ages since we've been there together.

Mason raises an eyebrow. "You in, Munroe?"

"Wouldn't miss it." It'll be good to unwind and shoot the shit. No business talk, no pressure.

Shelby hangs back, checking her phone. I wait for the guys to file out, nodding to Rick that I'll catch up in a minute.

"Goodness gracious, what a day," she mutters.

"Couldn't agree more." My hands curl into fists.

Shelby's eyes track the movement. "Did you plagiarize that rapper's music, like the papers say?"

The question slams into me like a gut punch. "No, I, uh, of course not," I stammer as heat creeps up my neck. Great, now I sound guilty.

Shelby tilts her head, her expression unreadable. To her, I must be another item on her to-do list, sandwiched between "buy more printer ink" and "call the caterer."

"Being accused of theft is insulting. I spent sleepless nights crafting those tunes while we worked on a collaboration project." The words tumble out. "I thought we were friends."

Shelby studies me, but I see no judgment in her gaze, only interest.

"False accusations hurt and cause a lot of damage," she says evenly. "After watching you guys rehearse, and observing the dynamics between you all, I changed my opinion. I believe you."

"The thought of people questioning my integrity—" I trail off, shaking my head. Something in me uncoils in relief. I barely know this woman, but her faith in me means so much. "The guys are heading to grab a drink. Wanna join us?"

Shelby seems surprised I've asked her. "Thanks, but I'll pass."

Ouch. I try not to let my smile falter. "C'mon, one drink won't hurt."

Shelby slings her bag over her shoulder. "I appreciate the offer but prefer to keep things professional."

She's all business and I respect that. "Another time," I say lightly, hiding my disappointment as I open the door. "After you."

Shelby nods and hurries past without looking at me. We've got a long tour ahead of us—plenty of time to get to know each other better.

This is only the start of our journey. The tour is a massive undertaking and it is slowly beginning to take shape. It's time to bid farewell to the studio. We're heading to Denver, and in a week's time, we'll be performing live for our fans.

Chapter 3
Shelby

One Week Later

The stadium hums with anticipation as the crowd waits for Soul Obsession to take the stage. I pace backstage, phone glued to my ear, juggling tasks like I'm part Ringling Brothers, part Wonder Woman. My nerves are shot, and my patience is on vacation in the Bahamas without me.

I had everything planned out perfectly. But the broken-down tour bus outside the stadium is a reminder that chaos is always a step away. It's my job to ensure the magic on stage isn't disturbed by the mayhem behind the scenes.

Tonight is the final concert in Denver. Apart from the bus-tastrophe, the shows have been exceptional. The "boyband" of ten years ago have matured into a testosterone-laden "manband"—their voices a little more gravely, their demeanor a little more relaxed and free onstage.

All these things have only made them more attractive to their thousands of adoring fans, judging by the swooning and panty-throwing over the last three nights.

Jameson appears at my side, signature smirk in place but I don't look up from my tablet. "Nervous?"

"I don't get nervous," I reply, marking another item off my list marked "Denver Shows."

"Even your first week of shows with us?"

"Another day on the job," I say with a shrug.

Jameson grins. "Cool as a cucumber."

My stomach is a knot of anxiety, but I'd never let it show.

Jameson is leaning against the wall, watching me. "Are we all set for Phoenix tomorrow?"

I swipe to a new screen. "Of course," I reply without looking up.

"Great. Don't need to be rushing all over the morning after a show."

"The hotel is three blocks from the venue." My tone makes it clear I've got it under control.

Jameson runs a hand through his hair. The weight of his gaze prickles my skin. "Don't think anyone else could wrangle this madness like you do."

"I'm only doing my job," I repeat.

He winks, a flirtatious glint in his eyes. "You do it damn well."

My cheeks grow warm, and I quickly look away. Jameson's flirty banter and lingering looks are distracting. I need to keep my focus, despite his charm offensive. Jameson is off-limits.

"Two minutes to stage!" a voice calls.

Jameson leans in. "Wish me luck?"

"Break a leg. Now go rock that stage."

He laughs and joins the others. Soul Obsession takes the stage, quickly captivating the crowd. Thousands of fans are cheering, unaware of any issues behind the scenes.

I glance at my watch and race outside to where the broken-down tour bus is parked and waiting for the tow truck. The bus driver, gesturing towards the bus, is arguing with the roadies, his wrinkled forehead and downturned mouth signaling his frustration.

One roadie pulls off his cap, runs his hands through his hair, and jams the cap back on, while another is muttering under his breath and kicking gravel.

I check my phone and see a notification. "The replacement bus should be here in an hour," I inform the driver.

The driver, a burly man with a full beard and strong hands, nods stoically as I give him the news. I lean against the bus, closing my eyes and finding a moment of relief from the weight of my responsibilities.

I'm in charge of coordinating flights, tour buses, and dressing room demands for this world-famous band. It's no joke—constant travel, cramped quarters, and no personal space.

If the band doesn't arrive at their next venue on time, if luggage gets lost, or if flights are delayed—it all falls on my shoulders. But I have no time for doubts or fears.

There are too many people counting on me for support. And with the media watching every move, eager to report on any scandal I can't afford any missteps.

Headlights swing into the parking lot—it's the tow truck. I wave them over, relieved of one less thing to worry about. The bus gets hooked to the tow truck, its wheels lifting off the ground. Right on time.

I give the new driver a thumbs up and check my phone for any last-minute alerts or crises needing attention. My phone remains silent. Everything is running smoothly again.

Brushing past roadies as they maneuver equipment, I make my way backstage to catch the rest of the show. I weave among them, narrowly avoiding colliding with a sound guy whose headset sits atop his curls like a makeshift crown.

Security guards, towering over my five-foot-four stature, give a nod of permission. My swift stride and unflinching gaze leave no room for doubt—I belong here.

It's hard to believe I'm part of a world tour. Me, little Shelby Fitzgerald from Blackthorne, Texas.

I scan the sea of faces, overwhelmed by the chaos and noise. It's a scene I'm growing accustomed to, but tonight, a familiar face catches my eye—Chastity.

I wasn't sure if she would make it to the Denver concerts due to her job with kids with additional needs. Ireland mentioned it was difficult for her to take time off, but I'm glad she wrangled it.

We met up at the after show following the first concert and had breakfast together the following morning. I'm not sure who was more surprised when Xander asked her on a date–him or her!

My gaze snags on Xander now as he stands side-stage, his gaze fixed on Chastity. Unless I'm mistaken, there's a whole lot of chemistry going on there.

My friend waves at me from the front row, a wide grin splitting her face. She's a beacon in the dark, her fiery hair glowing under the stage lights. I mirror her smile, relief flooding through me. Seeing her amidst all these strangers is like an anchor grounding me, reminding me of home.

I hadn't realized how much I needed to see a friendly face until this moment. Chastity waves at me again between songs and mouths, 'thank you' across the distance.

Her joy is palpable, and serves as a reminder—this is why we do what we do—to make people happy. I return her grin and blow her a kiss. I hope we get to spend more time together in the future.

Suddenly, there's movement at my side—Jameson strides toward me, sweat beading his forehead. He grabs a towel to mop his brow. "How we doing?"

"We're good," I reply, although "we" feels strange on my tongue because they're the ones performing.

He follows my gaze out into the crowd and spots Chastity. "Chastity is a friend of yours? I've spoken to her several times. She's a great gal."

"Yeah," I say with pride swelling in my chest. "She teaches kids with special needs back home."

"That's cool. Xander told me about her the other night. The world needs more people like your friend." Jameson nods approvingly before returning his attention to me, pinning me with his intense gaze. "And more people like you. You've been killing it on this tour."

My eyebrow arches, concealing my astonishment. A small surge of pride bubbles up at the praise. Jameson's praise shouldn't matter as much as it does, but I can't deny that he affects me in ways I've never experienced.

It's a heady sensation, and a little unsettling. I'm a practical gal. My life is organized and carefully mapped out. I don't have room or time for the chaos that would come with getting involved with a pop star.

I pull myself up short. *Hold up there, Shelby. Where did that thought come from?*

My relationship with Jameson is strictly professional. I don't notice his broad shoulders, melting dark eyes, or his intrinsic charm. Nope. Completely unaffected.

Jameson tosses his towel aside and heads back toward the stage with his signature cocky swagger. The crowd noise reaches a fever pitch. The band is feeding off the fans' infectious enthusiasm. I tap my foot along to the music, watching Jameson with rapt attention. I can't take my eyes off him. He's undeniably gorgeous, effortlessly commanding the crowd's attention with his dance moves and charm.

There's more to him than looks–a sensitivity beneath the polished pop star exterior. But I can't imagine what it would be like to date someone famous. Constant drama, invasive gossip rags, and zero privacy? No thanks. Give me a spreadsheet over a tabloid any day.

Jameson's voice wraps around me, at times angelic, at others gritty and raw. When he catches my eye our connection surges between us. It's so strong, I almost take a step toward him.

Okay–not as unaffected as I'd like to believe. *Focus, Shelby*. I was hired to manage the logistics of this circus, not join it.

I join in with the rest of the crowd, belting out the lyrics to all the biggest hits. My heart swells, caught up in the magic of this moment.

The final notes fade and my ears ring in the sudden silence. But then, thunderous applause erupts and I cheer along with the audience. The band clasps hands and takes a bow, waving appreciatively before leaving the stage.

This concert will be etched in my memory forever. At this moment, I realize the weight of everything I want but cannot have.

It doesn't matter how interesting I find the man behind the pop star persona because Jameson Munroe is off-limits. I'm here to do a job—not to swoon over a celebrity. No matter how sweetly he smiles at me. Or the heated intensity of his gaze.

After the show, I push open the door to the green room. The guys are sprawled across the couches, buzzing off the high of another energetic performance.

Empty water bottles and food containers litter the tables. The smell of hairspray and cologne hangs in the air.

Across the room, Jameson is crouched near the wall with his hand clenched firmly around his cell. His brows are furrowed and his shoulders are tense as he studies me.

His dark eyes trail over me slowly, and something flickers in his expression. Interest? Curiosity? An unexpected flutter stirs in my chest.

Asher cracks open a beer, raising it in the air when he sees me. "There she is! The woman of the hour!"

A chorus of thanks rings out as the backstage party kicks into high gear.

"Just doing my job." I give my standard reply. "The replacement bus will be ready in twenty minutes."

Rick pauses momentarily as he lines up rows of tequila shots. "To Shelby, for saving our asses when the tour bus broke down!"

He offers me a shot, but I hold up a hand to stop him. I want to review some specs before bed. "As fun as this looks, don't you guys have a radio interview at 8 AM?"

Jax grabs a beer and holds it out to me. "One drink won't derail your schedule."

I hesitate, glancing between the drinks and the rowdy, euphoric band members. The adrenaline coursing through me makes the shot tempting, and the couch does look comfortable.

"Maybe just one," I concede, sitting gingerly on the edge of the couch.

"We appreciate you holding it all together," Rick says warmly.

Jameson jumps onto the couch next to me. "Come on, you deserve a reward. A celebratory drink." Laughter lines crinkle at the corners of his eyes, giving him a boyish charm.

My cheeks heat. "The VIP tickets were reward enough. Thank you."

Jameson drapes his arm casually behind me. "It's great having Chastity here. I know Xander agrees," he says with a knowing smirk. "We're looking forward to meeting your sister and your other friends. Giving them the full VIP experience."

He stretches lazily, running a hand through his artfully tousled brown hair. The motion lifts his T-shirt, revealing a strip of toned abs. His proximity makes my skin prickle.

"What about you? Do you have a soft spot for our music?"

I raise an eyebrow. "I prefer music that won't damage my eardrums."

Jameson's eyes shine with interest. "Like?"

"Mongolian throat singing."

Jameson's husky laugh does peculiar things to my nether regions. "Mongolian throat singing?"

"It's calming."

I lock eyes with Jameson. His stare sends a rush of fire through me. *Screw it.* I grab a shot. It burns a heated trail down my throat, and warmth immediately spreads through my chest. I can't resist taking another one, caught up in the blissful sensation.

"Cheers to our girl!" Jameson shouts over the laughter and teasing.

While the guys chat and wind down after their performance, I mentally review my lengthy list of tasks for the following day. Weariness washes over me, and I zone out. My phone chimes with a notification, reminding me of tomorrow's schedule.

"Wild party tonight?" Jameson asks with a roguish grin.

I roll my eyes. "As if."

He nudges my shoulder playfully. "Maybe you need to relax and have some fun. Come out with us tonight."

I give him an incredulous look.

He leans closer. "You can't be all business all the time. Come on, first round's on me."

His breath tickles my cheek, making my heart skip. His nearness is affecting me more than I'm letting on. I bite my lip, tempted for a split second.

Jameson watches me, a grin playing on his lips. "Playing hard to get, huh? I like a challenge."

I push to my feet. "I'm not playing anything. I'm working."

Jameson holds up his hands in mock surrender. "Okay, okay. But the offer stands if you change your mind."

As my phone vibrates, I steal a quick look at the display. Rising, I sling my bag onto my shoulder. "I need to take this. Excuse me for a minute."

Jameson shoots me a flirtatious wink. The look in his eyes suggests desire simmering beneath the surface. However, my excitement quickly fades when the hotel manager at our next destination informs me that they have mistakenly double-booked our rooms.

I pace back and forth while I listen to his apologies and search frantically for solutions. This is a disaster.

After ten minutes of stress, I hang up with a shaky new plan in place.

Instead of returning to the green room, I find a quiet room, sink onto the couch, and kick off my shoes with a tired sigh. My feet ache after running around all day.

Rotating my aching neck, I try to release the tension coiled in my muscles and clear my thoughts of one achingly sexy band member.

Chapter 4
Shelby

My head snaps as Jameson strides in like he owns the place.

"Everything okay?" he asks as he sits across from me, propping his long legs casually on the coffee table.

I cough to clear my throat, distracted as I watch him fiddle with a pen with one hand while the other rests on his thigh. After watching him dance tonight, and seeing what he can do with those thighs, I struggle to stay in my seat.

"The hotel in Phoenix double-booked a couple of our rooms," I reply. "Thankfully, I had a few days' notice to get a boutique spot downtown so some of the crew

42

will have to stay there. It's less crowded, and has security."

"Do you ever stop working?"

"All in a day's work," I reply breezily, hoping he doesn't notice the hitch in my voice.

Jameson's eyes linger a beat too long. Something unspoken passes between us. My pulse quickens under his gaze.

Do your job, I remind myself. *No distractions allowed.*

Jameson's tone is low and smooth, a hint of gratitude coloring his words.

"I want to thank you," he begins, pausing for emphasis. "Privately. For everything you do behind the scenes. I don't know what I'd do without you."

His use of "I" instead of "we" catches my attention. I nod, unsure how to respond. We fall into a comfortable silence for a moment, allowing the background ambience to fill the void.

But as I look at Jameson closely, I see weariness etched into his features. Dark circles rim his eyes. My instincts kick in. "Is everything okay?"

Surprise flashes across Jameson's face at my question. "Yeah," he replies smoothly. "You know how it is—no rest for the wicked."

He tries brushing it off with a smirk, but making light of the situation doesn't cover the exhaustion in his voice or the tension bunching his shoulders. I can't imagine the stress of living under so much scrutiny.

I pause, wondering if I should push Jameson further about news on the scandal or let it drop. My job is to handle tour logistics, not pry into his personal drama. But something about his vulnerability pulls at my heart.

"I know we haven't known each other for long, but I'm here if you need someone to talk to," I offer gently.

Jameson gives me a small smile. "I appreciate that. This latest scandal...it's brought up a lot of stuff I thought I'd put behind me." He runs a hand through his hair and lets out a weary sigh. "I promised myself this tour would be different. I worked hard to build trust with the band and improve our image. But this scandal proves nothing's changed. It's the same bull-shit, but a different flavor."

My heart aches for the pain in his voice. "That must be difficult. I'm so sorry."

Jameson's eyes meet mine, open and searching. It's as if he's begging me to see beyond the cocky celebrity to the man underneath who needs a reprieve from the spotlight.

"I thought I finished playing this game, but the media won't let it go." He shakes his head, looking utterly exhausted. "I don't know how much more I can take. I need something to shift the focus. A buffer before this scandal tears me apart."

My heart breaks, seeing how heavily this is weighing on him. I wish I could whisk away the pain and pressure of his fame. But it's beyond my abilities or role here.

"I wish I could help take the heat off you somehow," I say softly.

Jameson hesitates, conflicting emotions playing across his face. He seems to be wrestling with a decision. Finally, he turns his earnest eyes to me. "There might be a way you can help. If you're up for it."

I tilt my head, surprised but curious. "Oh? What did you have in mind?"

He chuckles nervously, rubbing the back of his neck. "It's pretty out there. Hear me out before you shoot it down, okay?"

I nod for him to continue, intrigued by his sudden shyness.

Jameson takes a steadying breath. "So, one guaranteed way to get the media off my back would be if you posed as my new girlfriend."

My eyes widen in shock. That was the last thing I expected.

Seeing my reaction, he rushes to explain. "A fake relationship, just for the public. It would only have to be until the end of the tour. We'd go to some events, post cutesy pictures, and let the gossip blogs speculate. Give them something fresh to drool over."

I stare, unable to form words.

Jameson groans and drags a hand over his face. "God, that sounded insane out loud. Please don't think I'm some kind of creep."

I shake off my surprise. "No, no, it wasn't what I was expecting," I say carefully.

Jameson winces. "Forget I mentioned it. Bad idea. I'm grasping at straws here."

"Wait," I touch his arm. "I'm still processing, but will you explain why you think this could help?"

Hope flickers in Jameson's eyes. "You're not rejecting the idea?"

"I have concerns, naturally," I hedge. "But I want to help. Talk me through it."

Jameson nods, looking relieved. "Well, the media loves a new romance. If I show up on the red carpet with a gorgeous, charming girl who no one knows, they'll be all over it. It would give them something positive to report on." He lightly touches my hand. "And as we spend more public time together during the tour, it'll seem more and more plausible. Enough smoke to convince everyone there's a fire, so to speak."

I chew my lip thoughtfully. I can't deny his logic makes sense. From a publicity perspective, this scheme could work. And about a hundred ways it could go wrong.

"There are risks involved," I say carefully. "Scandals aside, won't people question why you'd start dating

47

someone who works for you? Won't it seem, I don't know, inappropriate?"

Jameson shakes his head. "Maybe at first. But your professionalism is iron-clad. Once they see us together, how smart and talented you are, questions about propriety will fade."

He squeezes my hand, eyes earnest. "The world needs to know the incredible woman I've found. This tour will show them that our relationship is real. That it goes beyond gossip and photos."

My pulse quickens at his words. His magnetic charm pulls people toward him, tugging at me like an irresistible force. Although I have doubts, some naive part of me wants to believe him. To trust this scheme could work. And what if something more comes of it?

A no-strings fling with Jameson seems less like a risk and more like an adventure. Falling for Jameson happens to other people, not me. I'm too grounded, too rational to lose my head.

It's not like I'm putting my heart on the line. This arrangement is purely business. This will be a fun story to tell with a wink and a smile, nothing more.

No. I force those dangerous thoughts from my mind. I'm here to do a job, not get swept up in a fantasy.

Sensing my hesitation, Jameson adds gently, "I know I'm asking a lot. You have every right to say no. But I promise I will never let this jeopardize your career. All it would take is a few public appearances and some cute photos to pique interest."

I sigh, knowing I'm about to cave. I hope I don't regret this decision for both our sakes. But there's one final thing I need to know before I agree to join him on this crazy adventure.

"Why me?"

He meets my eyes, his expression earnest. "You're the only one I trust to do this, Shelby. You see beyond the celebrity bullshit to the real me underneath. I need that now more than ever. Someone grounded who I can be myself around."

His heartfelt words soften my racing heart. He's trusting me. How can I turn my back in his time of need?

Jameson takes my silence as rejection. His shoulders slump in resignation. "I get it. It was too much to ask. Forget I mentioned anything."

Fern Fraser

Seeing him so sad stirs something protective in me. Before I can overthink it, I take his hand. The words are out of my mouth before I can stop them. "Jameson, wait. I'll do it."

Jameson's face lights up. "You will? You'll be my pretend girlfriend?"

I let out a shaky laugh. "I must be crazy, but if you think this will help, I'm in."

In a rush of excitement, he pulls me into a tight hug. "Shelby, thank you," he says fervently. "I promise, I'll make it as easy on you as possible."

My lips quirk. "Well, let's start by figuring out some ground rules."

Jameson nods, still grinning. "Lay 'em on me."

I cross my arms. "First rule–this arrangement is strictly business. No unnecessary PDAs."

Jameson smirks. "What if I can't resist your charm?"

I level him with a stern look. "I'm serious, Jameson. No inappropriate behavior."

He puts his hands up in surrender. "Okay, okay! I swear to be a gentleman."

I nod slowly as I take in his words. We're in agreement, then. I tap an uneven rhythm on the table. "Rule two–the fewer people who know about this, the less opportunity for it to fall apart."

Guilt washes over me at the thought of lying to people, especially to my mom, who somehow always knows the truth. I shift on the hard seat, the wood digging into my thighs.

Jameson rakes his fingers through his hair, his eyes clouded with uncertainty. "I don't feel comfortable keeping the band in the dark," he admits, shoulders slumping. "If they find out this relationship is a sham without us telling them, it could damage their trust."

Although I was trying to be professional, I breathe a little easier knowing he's on the same page about being honest with our inner circle. "You're right. Keeping up the act when with their support will make everything easier."

He gives my hand a grateful squeeze. It's brief, a friendly gesture, but the warm press of his palm sends a flutter through my chest. "I'll swear them to secrecy."

I quickly compose myself. "I should warn my mom I'm 'seeing someone." I glance down, contemplating a quick text to ease her and my dad into it. "If I lie, they'll want to meet you."

"I'd love to meet your folks." Jameson smiles.

The affection in his eyes makes my heart skip traitor-ously. *Get it together, Shelby. Strictly business.*

I smoothly redirect the conversation to mapping out public appearances. "Now, run me through what events you want to appear at. We'll start small–maybe a dinner date next weekend?"

Jameson agrees and begins to lay out a public timeline. As we talk logistics, my lingering doubts creep back in. Can I pull this off without jeopardizing my career? Or worse, my heart?

Every time my resolve wavers, Jameson smiles at me so hopefully. Even if I wanted to back out, I don't have the heart to disappoint him.

But all the while, a small voice in the back of my mind whispers, *Beware. You're playing with fire.*

Chapter 5
Jameson

SHELBY WILL BE HERE SOON. I quickly scan the hotel suite, making sure everything is perfect. After years in the spotlight, I should be immune to nerves. Yet my stomach flutters anxiously as I straighten the flatware for the hundredth time.

"Get it together," I mutter to myself. "It's a work meeting, not a first date."

A rap on the door announces Shelby's arrival. I dim the lights and straighten my collar before opening the door.

I flash her a crooked grin. "Hey, gorgeous. You made it."

Shelby's gaze goes to the dining table where takeout food is arranged on fancy platters beside lit candles. With soft jazz playing in the background, the atmosphere is intimate without being over-the-top romantic.

"Wow, you went all out."

I shrug, trying to act casual. Can't let her know how nervous I am. "I wanted you to feel comfortable. We can't be seen at a restaurant yet, and I—uh, want to make sure it feels authentic."

Authentic? That's the word I go with, genius? I mentally face-palm, rubbing the back of my neck as my face grows warm.

Shelby laughs. "Save it, Munroe. I'm here to work."

She slowly unbuttons her coat. She looks absolutely stunning in a figure-hugging teal dress and heels. Every part of her exudes confidence and sensuality. She's the epitome of my favorite sexy librarian fantasy.

Her sleek blonde hair is pulled into a high ponytail, tempting me to run my fingers through it. I resist the urge to nuzzle the smooth column of her throat, but my mind races with thoughts of peeling off her tight dress and discovering the hidden secrets beneath.

She clears her throat when she catches me staring. "Something smells amazing," she says, changing the subject.

"I hope you're hungry. I got a bunch of stuff from the Japanese place down the street. Wasn't sure what you'd be in the mood for, but I hope you're hungry." I pull out a chair for her. "Shall we?"

She thanks me, and gracefully takes her seat, as if guys do this sort of thing for her all the time. Considering how put-together she is, she's probably used to it. I don't want to think about other men doing this for her.

Once we're settled in our seats facing each other, I pour two glasses of wine. "Cheers to our fake dating adventure."

Shelby taps her glass to mine. "I'll drink to that."

We sip our wine while I think of something to say but my mind goes blank.

Shelby breaks the silence. "The crowds are enthusiastic. And reviews of the shows are great."

I nod. "Yeah, it's good to know the fans still want to hear our music."

Her mouth quirks. "Did you doubt it?"

"We all did," I admit. "Ten years is a long time, and the music industry has changed a lot."

"Good music stands the test of time. And you guys wrote great music with wonderful lyrics."

I stare at her for a moment, taking in the genuine light in her azure eyes. "Thanks. Means a lot coming from you. Particularly as a non-fan," I tease.

Shelby's husky chuckle slides down my spine and lands in my twitching cock. "I may glossed over the truth a little. I was a fan by association. Ireland played your albums morning, noon, and night."

I like that Shelby wasn't an avid fan. Somehow, it makes this connection, whatever it is, more genuine. She doesn't fawn all over us or throw around meaningless compliments. Although, I wouldn't mind her fawning all over *me* in the right situation.

Shelby asks thoughtful questions and seems genuinely interested in what I have to say as we talk. Soon we're swapping road stories and laughing over tales of disastrous gigs and unhinged fans.

I snag a piece of sushi, fumble with my chopsticks, and drop it into the sauce. I've done this a million times but my hands act like I'm defusing a bomb. Shelby stifles a laugh.

"My chopstick skills are rusty," I admit.

"Try holding them like this," she encourages, demonstrating a better grip. When I fumble, her fingers nimbly adjust my hold.

I grin. "That's way better."

Shelby smiles. "It takes practice. I learned working at a Japanese restaurant in college."

I make a mental note to brush up on my chopstick abilities later. Impressing Shelby has suddenly become a priority.

We continue eating, the conversation flowing comfortably. Shelby asks about my songwriting process. I'm struck by how intently she listens, like every word I say fascinates her.

Between bites, I sneak glances at how she delicately bites her lower lip in thought or sweeps back the loose strand of hair that keeps falling across her face.

Eventually, the conversation turns to practical matters.

"So when did we 'meet?'" I ask, making air quotes with my fingers.

She considers this, chopsticks paused mid-air. "Good question. We need to agree on a story and stick to it, or the press will sniff out inconsistencies like bloodhounds."

I nod, impressed by her approach. It's like she's done this a million times. "Okay, so what's our meet-cute? A serendipitous coffee shop run-in? Love at first sight across a crowded bar?"

Shelby tilts her head thoughtfully. "Hmm, maybe a year ago backstage at one of your shows? I was working at a VIP meet-and-greet. You were instantly dazzled by my efficient use of a clipboard and laminated signage."

I clutch my heart dramatically. "It's coming back to me. Our eyes met across the crowded room. You with your sexy headset mic and pristine lanyard. I knew you were the one."

Shelby snorts. "I'm swooning over here, Romeo."

I laugh, surprised by her deadpan humor. "Okay. How about we 'met' at a friend's wedding six months ago? The press eats up a good wedding romance," I say, snapping my fingers. "You were a bridesmaid, and I was a groomsman. You caught the bouquet. It was fate."

Shelby takes a sip of her wine. "That's pretty cliché."

I stroke my chin as if deep in thought. "Not the bit about you knocking out my tooth with that hard head of yours."

Shelby nearly spits out her wine before recovering. "That story might be crazy enough to work," she says when she can speak again.

Shelby fidgets with the stem of her wine glass. "So let's discuss logistics. We should map out public appearances, post photos together on social media, that sort of thing."

I lean back in the chair, trying to appear cool and collected. "Absolutely. How do you feel about holding hands at red-carpet events? Maybe a kiss on the cheek here and there.." I trail off at Shelby's raised eyebrow.

"Let's keep the PDA classy and minimal," she says briskly.

"Oh yeah, of course!" I backpedal. "You're absolutely right. We'll keep it friendly. Strictly PG." I let out an awkward cough.

Shelby's expression softens into a smile. "This fake relationship is tricky to navigate, but we'll figure it out together."

"Absolutely," I agree without hesitation. "You have my word."

"Good," she replies, her lips curling into a small, satisfied smile. "Because if we're going to pull this off, we need to trust each other completely."

The mood shifts back to casual as we continue chatting. We go back and forth, bouncing different strategies around as we craft a comprehensive fake dating game plan. Shelby comes up with creative ideas for "dates" we can reference. The more time we spend together, the more natural this feels.

"We should probably discuss social media too," Shelby continues, back in strategic mode. "Subtle posts, not overkill."

"Makes sense. I'll post a pic of that view earlier and tag the location as your hotel. Drop some hints," I say with a wink.

Shelby rolls her eyes but seems amused. She's cute when she pretends to be annoyed with me.

"Tell me about yourself, Shelby," I say. "Any deep, dark secrets I should know?"

Shelby smirks. "I had an unconventional upbringing."

I nod, waiting for a story about her sister.

"I hatched from an alien pod and was sent to infiltrate Earth."

I grin, pleasantly surprised by her quick wit. "I don't know if we can work that into our story, but I promise I won't tell anyone your secret."

Shelby isn't putting on an act for the sake of our deal—she's genuinely fun to be around. Her laughter loosens something in my chest. I want to get to know the real Shelby, not the uber-professional persona.

"Tell me more. What makes you tick?"

Shelby takes a sip of wine, considering the question. "I've always been career-focused. Even as a kid, I organized neighborhood plays and events. My sister says I should loosen up and live a little." She smiles wryly. "But I like having a plan. Makes me feel in control."

"And how's that working out for you, managing a bunch of reckless pop stars?" I joke.

Shelby laughs. "I'm up for the challenge."

Her confidence is impressive.

"What about you?" she asks. "There must be more to Jameson Munroe than tabloids let on."

"Tabloids got it wrong," I admit. "Music is still my passion. Nothing compares to being on stage. It's a rush."

Shelby wears a skeptical look. Is it because she doesn't believe me, or is she thinking the same thing I am? There is something better, and it involves her, and me, naked. Or not. I'll take what I can get if she'll let me get close enough.

But I change the subject, steering it back to where we began. I tell Shelby about my failed attempt at a solo career after Soul Obsession's breakup. The memory is bittersweet.

"I released an album and went on tour, but it was nothing like the stadiums we used to play."

"That sounds incredibly brave," Shelby says, her voice encouraging.

"Or stubborn." I shrug, trying to play it off, but Shelby's empathy is a balm to old wounds. "It was a reality check, though. So I shifted my focus to writing for others and collaborating with different artists."

"You traded the spotlight for behind-the-scenes creative fulfillment?" she summarizes.

"Pretty much. I'll always love performing, but I want my work to stand on its own merits too, you know?"

"Your songwriting is exceptional," Shelby says sincerely. "It's a gift."

"Thanks." Warmth hits my chest at her praise. Earning respect as a songwriter, not only as a performer, means everything. "That's why the plagiarism accusations hit so hard. It's like someone's trying to take that part of me away, you know?"

Shelby reaches across the table, her hand hovering as if she wants to offer comfort before she remembers our agreement. "I understand that desire to be appreciated for your skills."

"Those accusations are unfounded, Jameson. Anyone who knows your work can see that."

I'm impressed by how quickly she grasps my motivations. "I appreciate that."

I haven't opened up like this in a long time. Being around Shelby has my mind working in overdrive—in the best possible way. With her quick thinking and level-headed approach, this crazy scheme might just work.

I top up our wine glasses, reluctant for the evening to end. "Here's to a successful venture," I toast, raising my glass. *And here's to fake dating the most level-headed woman on the planet without screwing it up.*

We continue chatting as we eat. The conversation flows easily, punctuated by laughter. Shelby has a great sense of humor when she loosens up. But when she looks at me with those bright blue eyes, I want to get lost in them.

And when she licks her lips, I bite back a groan. There's nothing platonic about my feelings right now.

I almost forget we're supposedly on a "fake date" until Shelby pulls out her phone.

"We should take a few photos in case we need to authenticate our 'relationship' online," she suggests.

I slide my chair over and wrap an arm around Shelby's shoulder. She leans into me, holding up her phone.

"Say cheese," Shelby teases.

Our eyes meet and something electric passes between us. Without thinking, I lean in, drawn closer.

Shelby turns her head suddenly, clearing her throat. "Well, that should do it." She checks the photos and then drains her wine glass.

An awkward silence falls. I mentally kick myself. *Nice going, Munroe.*

"It's getting late." Shelby stands abruptly, all business again as she gathers her things. "Early start tomorrow. I should get going."

A hint of reluctance colors her voice. Or perhaps it's wishful thinking. What Shelby's taking on for me–the

scrutiny, the acting, the insane demand on her time—
is more than I have a right to ask of anyone.

Although I want to walk her to her room, it's too
much. So, I walk her to the door instead. "I appreciate
you stepping up like this."

Shelby takes her coat and gives me the playful half-
smile that's been making my heart do backflips all
evening. "What else are fake girlfriends for?"

She's one of a kind. I couldn't have asked for a better
partner in this madness. "I owe you big time."

Her smile widens. "I'll collect on that IOU when this
is all over."

I'm not ready for the night to be over. "Anything you
want. Name it and it's yours."

As Shelby stands hesitantly in the doorway, I want to
take her in my arms and never let go. I step closer.
Shelby's eyes flick to my lips and back up again. Is she
thinking about kissing me?

Shelby smiles and slips out the door. "Goodnight."

I lean against it, exhaling deeply. "Goodnight,
Shelby."

What am I getting myself into? Even as the thought crosses my mind, I already know it's too late. As I watch Shelby stride away, ponytail swinging behind her, I realize I'm already in too deep. Falling for my fake girlfriend will only bring heartache, yet I'm already dreading the day our fake relationship ends.

The only thing I can do now is to enjoy the ride but to spare making it worse for Shelby, I'll keep my true feelings to myself.

As I lay in bed, with the city lights casting shadows across the ceiling, I send her a quick text.

> Me: Had a great time tonight.
> Looking forward to our next "date!"

> Shelby: Me too.

I chuckle, typing a quick reply.

> ME: Maybe we could grab brunch?
> There are bound to be
> photographers around. Soft launch?

Three little dots appear and disappear. Silence.

Shit, I overstepped.

Shelby: Anything for the cause.

I stare at my phone for a long moment, a goofy grin spreading across my face. Yep, I'm a goner.

Me: C u at 10 AM in the lobby.
Sweet dreams!

I add the winky face emoji on impulse, hoping it comes across as friendly banter, not the longing I feel inside.

Shelby responds with a smiley face. As I drift off to sleep, my thoughts are filled with my blonde-haired, blue-eyed goddess.

Chapter 6
Jameson

THE NEXT MORNING I'm up before dawn. I skip my usual morning workout. Can't risk looking disheveled. Instead, I meticulously style my hair and shave twice in case I missed any stubble.

At 9:45, Shelby knocks on my door, looking effort-lessly chic in a flirty floral dress and strappy sandals. Her hair falls in soft waves around her shoulders.

"Ready for our big debut?" she asks brightly.

I whistle under my breath. "With you looking like that? Absolutely."

Shelby rolls her eyes but looks pleased. "Such a charmer."

69

My phone chimes with a text. "The car is here," I tell her. "It's showtime."

A discreet town car is waiting to whisk us to a hip brunch spot where we're likely to be spotted by paparazzi or fans. The restaurant is packed when we arrive. I made reservations under a false name to avoid tipping anyone off prematurely.

A server shows us to a table and we order food. I glance around but no one is paying particular attention to us yet. We chat casually as we wait, though I keep one eye peeled for any sign of photographers.

My mind races with fantasies of taking Shelby back to my room after brunch and exploring every inch of her perfect body. I take her hand in mine and bring it to my lips, brushing them against her skin.

"Let's forget about everything else for now," I whisper huskily, my eyes locked onto hers. "This is our date, just you and me."

A coy smile plays on her lips. "You're a dangerous tease, aren't you?"

"Oh, my gosh, is that Jameson Munroe?" a female voice suddenly squeals nearby.

I freeze. Here we go. I take a deep breath and squeeze Shelby's hand. Game on.

Two college-aged girls hover nervously beside our table clutching phones. "Sorry to bother you during your meal, but we're huge fans! Could we get a quick picture?"

I give them a charming smile. "Of course!" I sling an arm around Shelby's shoulders. "This is my girlfriend, Shelby." I give her a little side hug as I say it.

The girls' eyes widen. "No way. Your girlfriend? That's amazing!" They alternate between gaping at Shelby and snapping photos of us.

"It's still pretty new, so we'd appreciate you keeping the pics to yourselves for now," I say with faux shyness.

"Our lips are sealed!" one of them promises.

The girls return to their table, heads huddled together, giggling as they scroll through their photos.

Shelby raises her mimosa in a toast. "Nicely done. Those pics will be all over social media by tonight."

I bow with a flourish before sliding into the seat beside her.

Our food arrives and Shelby moans appreciatively as she takes a bite of her omelet. The sound sends a little jolt straight to my cock. *Get it together, man.*

I'm so focused on Shelby that I don't notice the paparazzo until his camera flashes in my face.

"Jameson! Who's the lovely lady?" he calls out.

My body tenses and adrenaline surges through my veins. Shelby, on the other hand, remains cool and collected, simply dabbing her lips with a napkin.

"Let's give him something to remember," she whispers confidently.

I rise from my seat and offer Shelby a hand. She stands gracefully and I pull her in close, wrapping my arm securely around her waist. Her response is flawless as she drapes an arm across my shoulders and flashes a warm, genuine smile at me.

We hold the pose for a few seconds as the camera clicks rapidly, capturing our perfectly staged moment for the world to see.

I smile and call, "No comment today, thanks, man!" as we retake our seats.

The photographer hovers momentarily, camera poised, before finally giving up and moving on.

"Wow. We did it." I can't keep the grin off my face. That went even better than I could've hoped.

Shelby lifts her mimosa again. "To us and the beginning of a beautiful pretend relationship," she proclaims with a playful sparkle in her eyes.

We finish our meal in high spirits, chatting and laughing. With the hard part over, I let myself sink into the moment. Being with Shelby is effortless, like we've known each other for years. I almost forget we're playing a role.

After brunch, we decide to take a stroll through a nearby park. The fresh air and exercise will do us good after that big meal. Plus, it provides an opportunity for more couple-y photos.

We meander along the walking paths, admiring the flowers beginning to bloom. When Shelby stops to smell them, I snap a candid photo with my phone.

"That's a keeper," I say, showing her the image.

Golden sunlight illuminates her face, eyes closed in bliss. She is radiant.

"Not bad," she agrees. "But we should take some selfies too."

I flip the camera and Shelby snuggles up beside me. We take a few smiling shots with the lilies behind us. Shelby insists we do some silly ones too, crossing our eyes and puffing out our cheeks.

"Let's take a short video too," she suggests. "To post on your Instagram story later."

I hit record and turn the camera on us. "Say hi, babe!"

"Hi, Instagram!" Shelby waves and blows a kiss at the camera.

I pan across the scenery and then back to us. Shelby leans in and plants an exaggerated smooch on my cheek.

I laugh, giving her a squeeze. "You're adorable."

She grins and nuzzles into my shoulder. Having her in my arms is so natural.

I end the recording and review the clip. "Perfect," I declare, knowing the fans will eat up this cute, candid moment.

We continue strolling, fingers loosely entwined until we come across a small pond. I set up my phone on a nearby rock and use the timer function to capture us sitting on the bench, my arm around Shelby's shoulder as we sit in the shade and feed the ducks.

Shelby shivers, and I drape my jacket over her shoulders. She snuggles into it and thanks me with a dazzling smile.

"Look at that masterpiece," she says, admiring the photo on my phone.

"It's all in the angles," I reply smugly, secretly pleased with her compliment.

After our spontaneous photoshoot, we dust ourselves off. Shelby's dress clings to her curves, accentuating every inch of her perfect body.

My fingers linger on her ass longer than necessary, as I brush away the stubborn piece of grass clinging to the back of her dress.

"It's clean now, thanks. If you keep going like that, the seams will tear."

Caught in the act, I quickly move away. Shelby chuckles. All too soon, we've looped back to where we entered the park. An ice cream truck is open for business with a small line of customers ahead of us.

"Fancy something sweet?"

Shelby gives me a playful smile and shakes her head. "I'm watching my figure for The Music Awards."

"You're already flawless," I tell her, making her blush and playfully hit my arm.

I pick up two cones and we make our way to the SUV, ready to head back to our hotel. I settle next to Shelby in the backseat.

"You were perfect," I say, holding up my hand for a high five. "The press is going to eat this up."

"We make a good team."

On the way to the hotel, we review the shots, choosing the best ones from our "date" to share online.

"That's enough for now," Shelby says after we've gathered a few. "We'll spread them out so it looks natural."

Her husky voice sends shivers down my spine. I lean closer, inhaling her sweet scent, and catch a glimpse of the delicate curve of her neck.

"I'll post a selfie today, maybe the video this evening," I suggest, knowing every post will have her beautiful face front and center. "Oh, and I should do an Instagram story of you leaving my hotel room in the same outfit."

Shelby's nose wrinkles. "The more breadcrumbs we leave, the more convincing it'll be."

She's adorable. If only she knew the power she holds over me with a simple flick of her perfectly manicured hand.

I post the selfie with a vague caption about brunch dates. As expected, it immediately receives thousands of likes and comments demanding details about my mystery girl.

When we arrive at the hotel, she pauses, turning to me, her cheeks slightly flushed. "I know we're pretending, but I had a great time today."

Warmth spreads through my chest. "Me too."

She smiles, blue eyes sparkling. "See you tomorrow? Phoenix here we come," she says enthusiastically.

Yeah, I'm hoping we'll both get to "come" in Phoenix. I clear my throat. "Definitely."

I close the door behind her with a smile. As crazy schemes go, this is turning out better than I could've imagined. Spending time with Shelby was easy. Natural. Fun.

And if a tiny part of me wishes it were real? Well, that's a dangerous thought I quickly push aside.

Chapter 7
Shelby

Three Days Later

OUR TOUR BUS purrs to a stop outside the Grand Hotel. I squint through the windshield at the throng of fans outside the hotel, their faces alight with excitement despite being pressed against the security barricades. Fans are the best people.

"Bloody hell, look at that one!" Mason points to a woman jumping up and down waving a sign.

Crue leans over for a better look. "What does it say? 'Jameson, Marry Me!' Ha! That's got to be the hundredth proposal you've had this month, eh, Munroe?"

79

Jameson chuckles, shaking his head. "I'm off the market."

Jax snorts, "You gonna break it to her gently, or shall I get on the PA system?"

Crue pretends to reach for the intercom."Attention everyone, Mr. Jameson Munroe is officially—"

"—fictionally," Jax interjects with a snicker.

"—spoken for!" Asher concludes with a flourish.

Mason leans over, pretending to wave solemnly to the fan. "Don't take it too hard, love. It's not you, it's the multi-million dollar celebrity fauxmance contract."

Jameson raises his hand to quiet the group. "Why can't you find true love through a contract?"

He looks at me for backup, but I merely raise an eyebrow, unfazed by their playful banter.

My fingers glide across my phone, quickly dialing the number for the hotel concierge. "This is Shelby Fitzgerald with Soul Obsession. We're outside, and there's quite a crowd waiting. I'm just confirming what we arranged about entering via the service entrance at the rear."

After receiving confirmation, I hang up and address our bus driver, directing him toward the back to avoid drawing attention.

Jameson grins at me from across the aisle, that bad-boy smirk in full force. "Always thinking ahead, huh, Fitzgerald?"

Jameson's goofy grin draws teasing comments from the other guys which is cute. The band knows about our 'arrangement,' and everyone's cool.

I shrug off his comment with a nod and a tight-lipped smile, like a Cheshire cat with a secret. But no one knows we're texting every night, sometimes even talking close to dawn.

The tour bus maneuvers into the narrow alley where the hotel's security guards are waiting for us. The bus door hisses open.

I step out into the humid evening, Jameson and the others filing out behind me. Security guards form a protective barrier as the assistants whisk our luggage away.

My heels click on the pavement as I reach the nondescript metal door leading into the hotel's service wing.

The hotel manager guides us into the hotel, the security guards trailing behind us like a safety net.

Once inside, the air conditioning hits me, and I suppress a shiver. Bright lights bounce off the polished marble of the grand entry.

The heady scent of fresh lilies perfumes the air. Jameson catches up with me as I follow the boys through the grand lobby of the high-end hotel.

Mason gapes at the grand crystal chandeliers and plush furnishings. "Blimey, Shelby, you always choose the poshest places for us to crash."

"Thank you," I reply simply.

Jameson gives me a knowing look before letting out a hearty laugh. "You've got a real talent for this, Shelby."

I give him a wry smile and check my watch. "Let's check in before the mob breaks in, okay?"

I trail behind Jameson, his lanky frame resting against the counter. The pretty clerk at the front desk perks up when she sees the band, her eyes locking on Jameson.

"Oh my gosh, Soul Obsession! I'm your biggest fan!" Her cherry-red lips part into a bright smile, her professionalism momentarily slipping.

Jameson flashes his signature crooked grin, clearly enjoying the attention. The clerk, who can't be more than twenty, blushes and bats her eyelashes.

I clear my throat pointedly. "We have reservations under Eclipse Entertainment," I say in my most authoritative voice.

"Of course. One moment, please," the clerk replies, barely glancing at me before returning her gaze to Jameson. Her cherry-red lips part into a bright smile, her professionalism momentarily slipping.

"Mr. Munroe, I can't believe I'm really talking to you! Your music is like the soundtrack to my life!" She's young, maybe too young to know better. "It would be so amazing if I could get a quick selfie with you," the clerk pleads, batting her mascara-coated lashes.

Jameson happily obliges, leaning in closer. "What's your name?"

"Tessa." She drapes herself over the counter to snap a photo on her phone, giving Jameson a not-so-subtle glance down her blouse.

"Anything for a fan," he says smoothly as Tessa gushes about her favorite Soul Obsession songs.

"That's awesome, Tessa. Thanks for the support."

Tessa's giggle is sickly sweet and fawning, ignoring the growing line of impatient guests.

"Sorry for the wait, folks. I can't believe it's really Soul Obsession standing here!" she gushes. "I've been a fan since I was fifteen. I can't believe you're back together."

The other guys chuckle, elbowing Jameson playfully.

I roll my eyes skyward, feigning disinterest. But inside is a churning mess of irritation and something dangerously close to jealousy. I can't be jealous. It's an act—this whole thing is an act.

"Goodness gracious," I mutter under my breath, feeling a prickle of irritation. I'm tapping my foot impatiently, reminding myself to remain detached, but this fan encounter is slowing down check-in.

When Tessa giggles at something Jameson says, my hands ball into fists.

"Excuse me, miss, but we're on a tight schedule," I say sharply. "I'd appreciate it if you could finish checking us in."

She glances at me dismissively before turning her attention back to Jameson. The nerve of this girl. I shouldn't care, but I can't deny the flare of jealousy in my gut.

"Here are your keys," Tessa coos. Her fingers 'accidentally' brush Jameson's hand.

Jameson smiles. He's only playing along, I tell myself, trying to smother the green-eyed monster rearing its ugly head. It's all part of his charm.

I wish he hadn't smiled at Tessa because she leans in, dropping her voice for Jameson's ears. Except I'm within earshot.

"If you need anything—anything at all—I finish work at ten." Tessa presses a card into Jameson's palm.

A bold move. I see red. Something deep inside me snaps and I storm over to Tessa's desk, snatching the card from her perfectly manicured claws. "Mr. Munroe won't need your assistance because I'm handling all his requests," I tell her with an icy smile.

Tessa's eyes widen in surprise, a slight blush creeping onto her cheeks. "My apologies."

I find Jameson's arm instinctively, my grip firm, claiming him as mine. Seeing the clerk's disappointed face is more gratifying than I care to admit.

As I lead Jameson away from the desk, he drops his voice so only I can hear. "I love it when you call me 'babe.'"

I don't know if I want to slap him or kiss the smirk right off his handsome face. I drop his arm, smoothing my hair self-consciously. "I don't know what came over me," I mumble, embarrassed by my sudden outburst.

Our eyes lock, and Jameson's dark gaze betrays nothing. "I'm not complaining. I could get used to it."

Jameson's intense gaze makes me feel both exhilarated and uneasy. I can't quite decipher the emotions behind his dark eyes, and it leaves me unsettled.

This is dangerous territory, but I've started down this path and don't know if I can turn back.

"Hey, Xander. It looks like you're out of a job. Jameson's got himself a new bodyguard," Asher jokes, nodding in my direction.

The guys exchange amused glances at my brazen display. They've noticed my reaction. My possessiveness. I don't care what people think of me. Not when Jameson looks at me like I'm the only thing he sees.

As we turn to leave, a camera flash blinds us. My gaze snaps to the source.

Paparazzi! Suddenly, photographers flood the lobby, snapping pictures and shouting at Jameson.

I freeze as camera flashes blind me, feeling utterly exposed. My first instinct is to shield my face from the invasive lenses, which only seems to fuel their excitement. Now, my petty outburst will be splashed across trashy gossip sites.

"Jameson! Over here!"

"Jameson! Who's your mystery girl?"

"Are you two dating?"

"How long have you been together?"

"Did you steal those songs, Jameson?"

Questions barrage us from all sides, invasive and relentless. My stomach clenches. I signed up for this, but that doesn't make it any less daunting.

Panic claws at my throat as I scan the lobby for an escape route.

Jameson reacts quickly. His hand finds mine in the chaos—a lifeline in the stormy sea of flashing cameras and prying eyes. His grip is firm, unexpectedly warm. "This way," he urges.

Keeping a firm grasp on my hand, he pulls me through the crowd, shielding me.

"Where did they all come from?" I gasp, momentarily blinded by the assault–this isn't a couple of paparazzi–it's an ambush.

"Must've been a tip-off," Jameson growls, his usual flirtatious demeanor replaced by a protective edge that sends an unexpected shiver down my spine.

"Let's make a run for it," he says, a rebel spark lighting up those brooding brown eyes. Trust Jameson to turn an escape into an action movie scene.

His hand enfolds mine, strong and assertive. He pulls me close, our fingers entwined—an intimate gesture. And oddly enough, it doesn't feel like part of the act. My heart is racing. The feeling of his palm pressed to mine awakens a flurry in my chest. I force myself to focus.

The lobby is packed with reporters shouting questions. Jameson and I weave through the crowded area, hands clasped as he leads us toward the elevator. My heart races, only partly due to the adrenaline.

In my haste, I'm not paying attention to my surroundings. As we approach the elevator bay, I brush too close to a woman clutching an oversized handbag. As she whips around, the bags' sharp metal clasp catches my delicate blouse.

Time slows. I watch in mute horror as the rip extends across the front of my blouse in a jagged line. If it continues, my sheer lace bra–or worse–will be exposed to all the cameras trained on us. Hot panic washes over me.

Photos of this wardrobe malfunction will be plastered across the internet in seconds.

Jameson's head whips back at my gasp, eyes locking on the wardrobe malfunction about to turn humiliatingly public. He swiftly shrugs off his jacket and drapes it around my shoulders, covering the torn blouse from view.

I pull the jacket closed, flashing Jameson a grateful look. Face burning, I grip the jacket with white knuckles.

"I've got you. Stay close," he urges under his breath.

Desperate to escape, my mind kicks into logistics mode.

"The staff offices are usually empty this time of day," I suggest breathlessly, picturing the hotel's maze of corridors. The shouts of the press grow closer.

"No time." Jameson glances over his shoulder, shaking his head as he pulls me in the opposite direction. "Trust me. I've done this before."

I try to bury the pang of jealousy, imagining other women he's had adventures with. I know the score. As we careen around a corner, we arrive at a dead end.

I huff in frustration, but Jameson tugs my hand. He races toward a recessed doorway, twists the handle, and ushers me inside, using the phone's flashlight to guide us.

We tumble into semidarkness, the door clicking shut and enveloping us in an eerie hush. In the phone's glow, I see Jameson's face, intent on listening to the commotion outside. Acting on instinct, I pull my phone from my pocket and silence it, stopping its incessant buzzing against my leg. A flicker of an impressed smile teases his lips. Without a word, he follows suit, extinguishing his own screen.

As my eyes adjust, I take in our surroundings–shelves stacked high with neatly folded sheets, duvets, and towels. The overpowering scent of fabric softener hangs heavy in the air. We stand in sudden darkness, the only sound the soft rustle of linens surrounding us.

Hyper aware of Jameson mere inches away, I steady my breathing and force my attention back to our predicament. Somewhere beyond the door, the paparazzi are waiting to pounce.

"That was close. Are you okay?" His voice rings with genuine concern.

I peek beneath the jacket, assessing the damage. A wardrobe mishap is trivial, but the media reaction could be explosive. The idea of my family seeing those photos makes me queasy.

I meet Jameson's eyes, suddenly overwhelmed. "Thank you. If they had gotten pictures of me like this–" I trail off, shuddering.

"Couldn't let you have a Janet Jackson moment."

The quip cuts the tension. I roll my eyes, laughing despite everything.

"I'm so sorry you got dragged into this circus. Once they smell blood, they go rabid for the shot."

"The media—how did they know?"

Jameson's eyes darken. "Probably that receptionist tipped them off, hoping for her fifteen minutes of fame."

I sigh, leaning back against a shelf. "Some professional I am, causing a scene like a jealous girlfriend."

Jameson's voice is low and teasing. "Didn't know you were the jealous type, Fitzgerald."

I meet his gaze with a scowl. "I'm not jealous."

He chuckles. "Sure thing, Fitzgerald. Whatever you say."

I roll my eyes. "I should apologize to that clerk. She didn't deserve my attitude."

Jameson reaches up to adjust a crooked stack of washcloths on the shelf above me. "I love seeing your possessive side."

He accidentally grazes my exposed breast. The heat of his touch is like a brand.

"Sorry, that wasn't...I didn't mean to—" he stammers.

"It's okay, we're...it's cramped in here."

We stand utterly still, neither pulling away. Jameson's face is inches from mine, his eyes burning with that intoxicating intensity.

As I hold my breath, my heart races. I'm acutely aware of Jameson's muscular frame pressed against me in the confined space.

"Shelby, I—"

"It's the adrenaline, right?" I cut him off, tension creeping into my voice. "We're caught up in the moment."

But even as I say the words, I know it's more. The air between us is thick with unspoken words.

"To hell with it," I breathe.

In this tiny, towel-lined cocoon, the rules don't apply. Gripping his collar, I pull him close until our lips meet. The kiss is tentative at first, the briefest whisper. Jameson's arms encircle me tightly as my fingers twist into his hair.

I savor this stolen moment before we return to the real world and our convoluted charade. Nothing exists but this moment and us, kissing each other fiercely in the shadows.

It's only us, the scent of laundry detergent, and the taste of his kiss. And for now, it's enough.

I'm not sure which of us breaks the kiss first when the voices outside finally fade into silence. We stand wrapped in each other's arms, breathing raggedly, faces still inches apart. Jameson brushes hair from my cheek, his touch impossibly tender. "Does this change things between us?"

"I don't know but I'm not ready for it to end."

"A little longer sounds good to me."

His lips find mine again, more urgently this time.

Chapter 8

Shelby

WE STUMBLE around the cramped linen closet, our lips locked. Urgency consumes us, the shelves rattling with each movement. His kisses are like liquid fire, igniting every inch of my body. I eagerly wrap my legs around him, my core throbbing with desire for more of his touch.

"Jameson," I whisper between kisses, my fingers sinking into his hair when he nips at my bottom lip.

His breath is warm in my ear, sending shivers down my spine and making me ache for him even more.

"Fuck, you feel so good," he growls, pressing me against the wall, asserting dominance as his hand pins mine above my head. "I could do this all night."

Fern Fraser

His other hand roams freely over my body, teasing and tantalizing every inch he can reach. "I love how needy you are for me."

The butterflies in my stomach turn into a wild frenzy as his skilled fingers trace patterns on my skin through the flimsy fabric of my torn blouse. Damn, this man knows how to make me feel alive. Our kisses become more frantic as he grinds his hips against my pelvis.

And then he's tugging my blouse over my head and fumbling with the clasp of my bra—it hits the floor with a soft whoosh.

Jameson is looking down at my exposed breasts. His eyes blaze. "So beautiful, all mine," he says, sending a spike of arousal through me.

I'm playing with fire, but I want him to worship every inch of me. His lips trail hotly down my neck, sucking gently at the pulse point. I moan loudly as he teases a sensitive spot below my ear, making me weak with desire.

"You like that, baby?" Jameson rasps, his voice dripping with lust.

"Mmm," I nod, unable to find my voice.

"That's what I like to hear. I can't wait to discover every way to make you quiver."

He claims my lips, and my body tingles with anticipation as he unzips his pants.

"I can't wait to feel you wrapped around me," he murmurs, biting at my bottom lip.

"I can't believe this is happening, but don't you dare stop," I whisper into his ear. "I want to touch you."

I wrap my fingers around his hard length, stroking slowly, his skin smooth and hot. "Like that?" I ask, picking up the pace as he groans into my mouth.

"Faster," he rasps, grinding against me. "You smell so good, baby. I can't think straight when you touch me like that. Tell me what you want," he murmurs huskily against my jawbone, lips trailing lower.

"You," I reply without hesitation, pulling him closer, even though there's barely room left for us to maneuver. "I want you."

"God. Need to be inside you," he whispers, finding my clit through the lace of my panties and rubbing gentle circles. "Say it," he demands.

"I want you inside me," I pant, my hips grinding into his touch.

He grabs my hips roughly, and his heat presses against my core. I know what's coming next will change everything. But for now? Jameson Munroe makes me forget my doubts.

He chuckles darkly before pulling away and spinning me around to face the wall, pressing my hands against the wall as he tugs my panties down my legs.

Then, he lifts my skirt in one swift movement. The air hits my bare ass, sending shivers down my spine before he spreads my folds with his fingers.

"So fucking wet for me," he growls as he teases my entrance.

I moan in pleasure but also remember we need to use protection. "Do you have a condom?" I whisper.

"Don't worry, baby, I do. But damn, you feel so good I almost forgot."

His words send a thrill through me, knowing that he cares about our safety and pleasure. He slides it on slowly and I enjoy watching every move.

"Ready?" he asks, positioning himself behind me.

I'm not ashamed of how easily he's unraveling me. For once, I'm throwing caution to the wind and taking what I desire. "Always. But only for you."

"Shelby," he groans into my neck, teeth grazing softly before biting down gently on the skin there. With a harsh smack on my ass, he slides into me with one smooth thrust that sends lightning bolts straight to my core.

"Oh fuck," I gasp as he fills me completely.

I arch off the wall with a whimper when he finds just the right spot inside me over and over again. I can't believe how good this feels—hidden away where no one will find us. It's so unexpected, yet so right.

Our bodies press tightly together, and sweat beads on my back. He thrusts deeper, harder—like he's trying to drive both of us crazy, slamming his hips into me until we're fucking like animals in heat.

I bite my lip to stifle my cries, but I can't hold them back. Jameson twists my face, swallowing my moans with his mouth.

And then it hits me—an orgasm that leaves me gasping. My walls clench around him tighter as waves of pleasure crash into each other.

With a final thrust, Jameson stills behind me with a primal grunt, sinking his teeth into my shoulder.

We both pant heavily, hearts pounding. Our bodies slow gradually until we're no longer swaying with the aftershocks of our climaxes. Pressed together like we're the only thing keeping the other upright.

"You're amazing," he murmurs in my ear, pressing a kiss against my neck before pulling out. There's a soft zip as he tucks himself back into his pants. "That's so you won't forget me."

My skirt falls over my bare bottom, and a wide grin spreads across my face. "Forget you? I won't be able to walk straight for a week."

Jameson will never commit to an ordinary woman like me. This is physical attraction, not love. But as we stumble on shaky legs, his scent lingering on me, I don't regret it. In Jameson Munroe's arms, I feel desired and for a fleeting moment, I know what it is to be worshipped.

Jameson presses his ear to the door, listening intently. "Sounds like the coast might be clear."

"We should make a break for the guest elevators before they circle back."

I hesitate, not liking the uncertainty. Instead, I wake my phone and message Xander, our head of security.

> Stuck in a linen closet on the 7th floor. Paparazzi everywhere. Need discreet exit. Shelby

Message sent, I wait in taut silence.

My phone vibrates with Xander's reply:

> On my way. Don't move.

We pass the tense minutes listening to our synced breaths, the linen rustling with our subtle movements. Then come two quick raps at the door–our signal.

Jameson cracks it open, peering out before stepping aside for me to follow.

Xander's voice is low and steady. "All clear for now. Let's move."

We trail Xander swiftly through back corridors–the hidden veins of the hotel. He guides us to the elevator through the service corridor and takes us up a side staircase so we don't encounter other hotel guests.

While we're in the elevator, I check my phone. It's been vibrating, a relentless dance of pings and dings. It's the same for Jameson.

"Congratulations. We're trending," Jameson drawls, tipping his screen toward me.

Predictably, gossip sites have already picked up the story. I wince at the photos of Jameson pulling me through the crowd. In each shot, he shields me protectively. Beneath the headline *Soul Obsession's Jameson Caught Cozy with Mystery Woman,* commenters debate my identity.

I force a laugh. "We need damage control, stat."

"Damage? Look at this—it's PR gold." He waves his phone like a winning lottery ticket. "'Jameson Munroe's mystery girl finally revealed!' They're eating it up."

"Ugh, they caught my good side at least," I quip, trying to keep the mood light despite the sinking feeling in my stomach.

"You only have good sides," Jameson fires back, a flirtatious smirk playing on his lips.

Something warm blossoms in my chest, even as my brain screams caution. "Flattery will get you, well, actually, it might get you pretty far right now."

When we reach our floor, Xander advises us, "You should both stay low for tonight."

Jameson nods in agreement. "We'll talk later."

Xander heads off down the hall, and Jameson and I are left standing awkwardly outside my room.

Leaning against the opposite wall, Jameson runs a hand through his hair—a gesture I'm learning signifies his discomfort. "We need to talk about what just happened."

I avoid looking directly at him, scared of what I'll see in his eyes. Or what he'll see in mine. "We crossed a line."

Jameson nods, his jaw clenched. "I know."

Fear twists in my gut—fear of entanglement, fear of scrutiny, fear of caring too much. "It can't happen again. We need to keep things professional."

"Cool and professional," he echoes. He pushes off from the wall and closes the distance between us.

Fern Fraser

My chest tightens at his agreement—even though it's what I want to hear. "Right," I say, though it feels like swallowing shards of glass.

"Shelby–" Jameson pauses, hand resting on the doorknob without turning it.

"I know this is right," I say softly, willing him to believe it too. I meet his eyes and find them searching —perhaps for reassurance or regret; it's hard to tell which.

"Well, I guess this is goodnight then." After a long silence, he opens the door. "But Shelby?"

"Yes?"

"Sorry. Not sorry." He trails off with a wink—lightening the mood while also acknowledging the momentousness of what happened between us.

"Goodnight." Once in my room, I slide down the door, my adrenaline fading to exhaustion.

With a groan, I kick off my heels. One thought keeps circling through my mind–the lingering sensation of Jameson's lips pressed urgently against mine in that dim, cramped closet. A reckless stolen moment I shouldn't dwell on but how can I forget? Because

104

Jameson makes me feel alive in ways I never knew were possible.

Trying to unwind, I pour a glass of wine from the minibar. My phone dings–a text from Jameson.

> Checking in to see how you're
> doing, beautiful. Let me know if you
> need anything. I'll be your knight in
> shining armor. XOXO

Goddamn it. He isn't playing fair! What happened to "cool and professional?"

Butterflies swarm my stomach. Ignoring the ache in my chest, I reply with a smiley face and hit send.

With a groan, I realize my defensive walls are rubble around Jameson. Although I promised myself I would pretend for the cameras and keep my heart in check, it's impossible.

For better or worse, Jameson's charm has breached my armor. My feelings for him are becoming real.

The problem is that Jameson explicitly chose me for this job because he could trust me to hold up my end of the deal without creating complications.

I owe it to him to keep my feelings to myself. I'll do my job perfectly, even if it means my heart ends up being torn to shreds.

I'm past the point of no return. I only hope I survive the freefall.

Chapter 9

Jameson

TODAY'S BAND meeting feels more like an intervention than a strategy session. I slump into the plush leather couch in our makeshift conference room, running my hands through my hair in frustration. The guys are sprawled in various states of exhaustion from the demands of touring.

While the tour is going great, my relationship with Shelby is blowing up all over social media. Dating me, even pretending to date me, has brought more chaos into her life than she bargained for. She's a professional, not some sidekick in my narrative of damage control.

The incoming calls and messages are coming nonstop. I silently toss my phone onto the glass coffee table

107

with an irritated huff. "I can't deal with this right now," I mutter.

Jax, Asher, and Crue nod sympathetically.

"I'd go crazy too if I were you," Asher says.

"It's insane how quickly this thing with Shelby blew up," Crue adds, shaking his head. "Every entertainment site is talking about you guys."

"People love Shelby. She's gaining a cult following," Jax muses.

I grimace, scrubbing a hand down my face. I knew there would be pressure but I never wanted Shelby to become a tabloid target.

I never should have asked her to do this. It was selfish of me to think she could step into the role of pretend girlfriend without it massively disrupting her life.

A sharp elbow in my ribs from Jax brings me back to the conversation. "Earth to Jameson!"

I blink, realizing the guys are all staring at me expectantly. "Uh, sorry, what?"

Rick jumps right back into reviewing our upcoming tour schedule, rattling off cities and venues. *Get it together, Munroe.*

I need to focus on the band meeting, not daydream about exploring whatever is brewing between me and Shelby. But my mind wanders again, my leg jiggling with excess energy under the table.

Right on cue, the conference room door opens, and Shelby walks in. I see the slight tightening around her eyes, the way she holds her phone like it's a grenade about to go off.

I watch as she sits across from me, looking immaculate in one of her signature skirt suits. She taps her fingers on the table—a Morse code for stress, maybe? Or impatience?

"How are you holding up, Shelby?" Rick asks gently.

All eyes turn to her.

"I won't lie—it's overwhelming. But I'm fine," she replies crisply, but her voice lacks confidence.

Something inside me clenches at her admission. "It's too much."

Shelby's gaze meets mine. "I signed up to help out."

Guilt twists in my gut. "But not for the frenzy surrounding us. I'm sorry for dragging you into this mess. If you want to back out, say the word and we'll issue a statement."

The band members shift uncomfortably in their seats; they've seen plenty of women come and go from my life—none stuck around when things got tough.

"I'm not backing out," Shelby declares firmly.

Relief floods through me so fast I almost feel dizzy with it. I nod gratefully at her across the table. Is this what a genuine partnership looks like?

"We appreciate you dealing with this," Rick says. "Jameson especially. This arrangement is already helping his image. And helping the band. Sales are up eighty percent overnight."

"Great news! That'll increase after we attend The Music Awards," she says enthusiastically, giving Rick a quick high-five.

The guilt sits like a weight in my stomach. I naively thought this arrangement would be easy—a quick fix to repair my image, but that was before I got to know her.

I've never met anyone like her before. She's principled, whip-smart, and caring. What really gets to me is how Shelby sees me as a real person, not as a commodity. It's always been that way for me, it happens when you find fame so young. Shelby isn't like that.

The more I get to know her, the more I want to unravel all her layers. And after our little impromptu sex fest in the linen closet, my feelings for Shelby have grown exponentially.

I've never wanted someone so badly, not just sexually, but on every level. But I agreed to keep things professional, and it's getting harder.

Like my cock every time I think of Shelby. My heart, on the other hand, is softening for my blonde beauty. *Fuck.*

During the rest of the meeting, my gaze drifts to Shelby, intently reviewing some paperwork. A strand of hair has fallen loose from her ponytail, and it takes all my willpower not to reach over and tuck it behind her ear. I force myself to look away before she notices me staring.

Doubt creeps in, and I rake my hand roughly through my hair. How will I convince Shelby to take a chance on me? Not as a pretend boyfriend but as someone reliable, a man she can build a life with.

I'm impulsive at the best of times. My track record with relationships is rocky, to put it mildly. The media spotlight is always glaring, ready to expose my flaws.

My leg bounces faster under the table. The rest of the meeting drags on, but when Rick finally wraps things up, I make a beeline for Shelby before she can slip away.

"Wait up a sec," I say, catching her arm. She turns, eyebrow raised expectantly. "Can we talk for a minute? In private?"

Shelby glances at my hand on her arm before meeting my eyes. "Sure."

I lead her into the hallway, out of earshot from the guys. She waits expectantly, one hand placed on her hip. Although she smiles politely, I sense wariness. Meanwhile, my palm tingles from her soft skin under my fingertips.

Shoving my hands in my pockets, I say, "I want to apologize. I never expected this would become such a big media spectacle so quickly. You didn't sign up for this level of scrutiny, and I feel responsible."

"You don't need to apologize," Shelby replies, her expression softening. "I knew what I was getting into when I agreed to this. My eyes were wide open."

"Still, you've been thrown into the spotlight. It isn't easy."

Shelby shrugs. "It's a shock to the system, but I don't regret it."

I want her to know she can be honest with me. "You're allowed to have boundaries. Just say the word if it ever gets to be too much."

Her unwavering gaze meets mine. "I'm committed to seeing this through if you are."

I nod slowly, unable to ignore the surge of emotions coursing through me. I don't know what I've done to deserve Shelby's loyalty, but I'm falling for her. Hard.

"Shelby, you're–" I trail off, unable to find the words.

Before I can stop myself, I reach for her, cradling her face. I smooth my thumbs over the delicate skin of her cheekbones, struck by her beauty. I dip my head, slowly telegraphing my movements–I'm going to kiss her.

A sudden throat-clearing and choked cough startles us apart. I quickly turn to see Rick standing in the doorway of the conference room. "We need to get to a TV interview."

"Shit," I mutter, cursing the interruption.

Cheeks flushed, Shelby strides past Rick without giving me a backward glance. As I watch Shelby walk away, the subtle sway of her hips holds my attention but I force myself to turn away.

Yeah, taking things slow with Shelby is going to be harder than I expected. But I'm determined to win her over and convince her we belong together.

No matter what it takes.

Shelby

Over the next few weeks, Jameson and I perfect our fake relationship. Small touches, loving looks, sweet social media posts—we have everyone convinced. In private, we talk for hours, growing truly close.

On the rare evenings we have off, we order room service and watch movies in Jameson's hotel suite. Curled up on the couch in sweats while we laugh over old movies feels wonderfully domestic. No cameras, no performing, just us.

The lines between real and pretend blur. Each day, my feelings for him grow stronger. But Jameson maintains a respectful distance when we're alone.

Am I imagining his lingering looks and touches? Does he feel this, too?

We've been intimate. I know I said we should keep things professional, but I want more. And it scares me more than anything ever has.

Chapter 10
Jameson

A COUPLE OF DAYS PASS, and we're in a new city, preparing for another round of sold-out shows. In my dressing room backstage, I pace back and forth, psyching myself up for tonight's performance.

We never planned on becoming a boy band, but it became important to us and our fans. And it still is. Our fans are expecting a killer show, and I aim to please.

The walls tremble with the deafening roar of the crowd. This is the moment we've been waiting for. The familiar rush of adrenaline and nerves courses through me before every show.

It's time to become the international popstar heart-throb Jameson Munroe and give the fans what they came for. I take a deep breath, rolling my neck and shoulders to release the tension.

I should be focused on the setlist, the dance moves, and the adoring fans. But my mind keeps drifting to Shelby.

I used to be all for the no-strings fling—easier to keep your heart intact. My past relationships were shallow, and my fame felt hollow.

I'd given up on finding something real, but with Shelby, my smiles are genuine. My laughter isn't forced. Now, I crave the strings, the knots, the whole tangled mess of sharing my life, sharing me, with someone. With Shelby.

Rick saunters over with a knowing grin on his weath-ered face. "You've got that look again."

"Which look?"

"The one where you're five seconds from writing a ballad about a girl who's got your world spinning."

I scoff, rolling my eyes.

"I've seen the way you are around her. You're different. Real."

"Real, huh?" I muse. "That's a heavy word for something that started as a front."

"Believe me, it's rarer than an honest manager in this biz." Rick plops on the couch, quickly ripping open a bag of chips. "Sometimes the best things start from a fake situation. Happens all the time on reality TV."

I frown and shake my head. "This isn't a TV show."

The band's unofficial philosopher shovels a handful of salty snacks into his mouth, crumbs scattering across his shirt. "Sometimes, it's okay to take a leap of faith," he mumbles.

"Thanks, Yoda." I crack a smile. "Is it that obvious?"

"I've seen how you look at her," Rick says. "And how she lights up around you when she thinks no one's paying attention."

I let out a long breath and the tension in my shoulders eases slightly. "Navigating all this is complicated."

Rick laughs. "Love is the ultimate complication. If you don't take a chance on her before this tour ends, you'll always wonder "what if.""

A soft knock at the dressing room door interrupts us before Shelby pokes her head in, flashing me a smile. She's stunning in a tight black dress and heels that I'd love nothing more than to peel off her later.

Shelby meets my gaze, a knowing smirk playing on her rosy lips. She's holding a bottle of blue electrolyte drink and a protein bar. "Thought you could use some fuel before the big show tonight."

She knows just how to take care of me. "You remembered."

"Special delivery for your favorite, huh?" Rick teases, wiggling his eyebrows suggestively before making his exit.

"Goodness gracious, you'd think they'd never seen someone bring a drink before," Shelby quips.

"Got to stay hydrated," I reply, taking the bottle from her delicate hand. I wrap my arms around her. "Have I told you how amazing you are?"

She laughs. "Only about a hundred times. But feel free to keep going."

I smirk, pulling her closer. Her scent is intoxicating—floral and feminine. "You look irresistible in that little black dress." I trail my hand down her back, feeling the smooth fabric against my skin. "The dress would look even better on the floor."

Shelby's eyes darken. "Why, Mr. Munroe, are you trying to seduce me?"

I nuzzle into her neck, relishing in the soft moan that escapes her lips. "Is it working?"

"Only if you promise to dance with me later," she purrs.

She raises an eyebrow suggestively. Something tells me tonight's show won't be the only thing heating up.

"And what if I want to do more than dance?" I ask, setting the snacks aside.

Anticipation coils tight in my gut at the memory of our frantic sex. Gripping her hips, I pull her firmly, walking her backward until she's pressed against the wall. Shelby kisses me back feverishly, our tongues tangling.

Her hands explore my chest and abs, tracing each ridge and plane. I shudder with pleasure, my body coming alive under her touch. I grasp her backside, squeezing gently. She rocks her hips against me instinctively, and I'm lost.

"We should stop," she gasps, breaking the kiss, even as her fingers trail under my shirt to trace my skin.

"I want you, Shelby," I groan, capturing her mouth again passionately.

"The show," she reminds me gently.

Her cheeks are flushed, and her lips swollen from our kisses. I lean in, brushing my nose against hers and smiling against her lips. "To be continued."

As I jog down the hallway, I glance back to see Shelby watching me, a secret smile on her lips. Tonight will be one for the record books because every note I sing will be for Shelby.

"Let's do this," I say to no one in particular and jog toward the stage, giving the crew high fives. The opening act is finishing up their set.

"Sixty seconds!" a stagehand calls.

I hear the opening chords of our first song. My band-mates are beside me, jumping and whooping, hyping each other up. We're ready to give these fans a killer show. We burst onto the stage, the bright lights momentarily blinding me.

The energy from the audience hits me like a tidal wave. I soak it in, coming alive under the spotlight. The guys are grinning, feeding off the energy. The adrenaline is kicking in now.

"Hey, you beautiful people!" I shout. "Let's make some noise!"

The familiar thrill courses through me as we launch into the first song. Muscle memory takes over, and I'm lost in the music. The crowd sings along, hands waving in time.

A few songs in, I spot Shelby side-stage with the other crew members. Our eyes meet, and she gives me a discreet thumbs up. I wink back quickly.

During the bridge of our biggest hit, I toss the mic aside and rip open my shirt. The crowd goes wild. I fall to my knees, belting out the emotional lyrics. Hands reach for me, and camera phones flash.

I lose myself in the music, channeling everything I feel for Shelby into my performance.

As we segue into a romantic ballad, I close my eyes and picture Shelby's face. Her touch, her kiss, the flame between us. I pour all my emotions into the songs.

Shelby's in the front row, dancing with abandon and laughing with her friends. Seeing the women having so much fun makes the effort worthwhile.

In our new song, 'So Yours,' I substitute the word 'baby' with Shelby. This heartfelt song about an unexpected love is a tribute to her.

Shelby looks surprised, then flushes slightly as her friends nudge her playfully. Shelby's eyes glisten under the stage lights. In this sea of thousands, it feels like we're the only two people here.

The song ends, and the crowd's cheers snap me back to reality. I grin, slightly bowing before launching into the next fast-paced hit.

We churn out song after song, keeping the energy high. Sweat drips down my back, but the exhaustion is sweet. By the end, we're breathless but exhilarated.

I linger on stage momentarily, looking out at the people who make this dream possible. Spotlights dance across ecstatic faces. Flowers and gifts litter the stage.

As we take our final bows, I hope Shelby knows how much her support has come to mean to me. With her endless patience, compassion, and strength, she's become my touchstone of calm in the chaos.

Backstage, I'm buzzing with adrenaline and giddy exhaustion. My bandmates are equally psyched, raving about the crowd's energy. I towel the sweat from my face when Shelby appears in the doorway.

"That was incredible!" she says, eyes bright. She gives me a quick hug, seeming flustered for a moment. "My friends and I had the best time."

"It was the least I could do. I'm glad you all had fun," I say.

Her friends' laughter echoes from down the hall.

"So, that song–" Shelby says, trailing off.

In the humming energy of the dressing room, I rub the back of my neck, suddenly self-conscious under her questioning gaze. "The song reminds me of you."

Shelby smiles softly, glancing down as if deciding how to respond.

"Shelby! There you are!" Her friends burst in, breaking the moment. "We're heading out to celebrate, you coming?" one asks brightly. Shelby hesitates, glancing at me.

"You all go on. I'll catch up," she tells her friends.

Shelby's friends are a lively bunch of women, always on their own adventures and making connections with the guys in the band and road crew.

As the tour progresses, and new friends join the tour, they're becoming ingrained in our group like permanent fixtures. Their voices fill the air with laughter and gossip as they make their exit.

Shelby turns back to me. "Thank you for the song. It means a lot that you would do that."

A surge of desire hits me. All I can think about is tearing off her clothes. Impulsively, my hand finds hers, lacing our fingers together.

Once we step into the dimly lit hallway leading to the band's dressing rooms, I pull her closer and press my body against hers, feeling her soft curves mold to mine.

I waste no time in pulling Shelby into a passionate kiss. Our mouths crash together in a messy kiss that has our tongues dueling and teeth nipping.

She tastes like fire and desire. I trail kisses along her jawline before nibbling gently on her earlobe. She tastes so good–sweat and arousal mixed together–it's intoxicating.

Our hands roam each other's bodies, desperate to feel every inch of skin. I trace the outline of her neck, her pulse racing beneath my fingertips.

We fall onto a stack of crates and I'm above her, fingers tangled in her hair. My cock is throbbing, desperate to be free, wishing we were naked.

"Do you want to ditch this party and go back to my place instead?"

Shelby's eyes widen and a mischievous smile plays on her lips. "I thought you'd never ask."

We leave the venue in a hurry, hailing a cab to take us to my place, our hands intertwined. Shelby texts the girls, telling them she'll catch up with them later.

Once inside, we barely make it to the bedroom, our need overriding anything else.

I guide her hand to my cock. "I need you," I whisper against her lips.

"All I need is you, Jameson."

Hearing those words in her husky voice is my undoing. "I can't deny you anything, baby," I whisper between kisses. I'm like a man possessed. I kiss her lips, her cheeks, and her forehead before returning to her lips. I'll never get enough.

"What do you want?" I whisper in her ear. "Tell me what you want, and I'll give it to you." Shelby has made huge sacrifices for me. There's nothing I won't do for her. Nothing. If she says she wants me to lasso the moon, I'll find a way to do it.

"You." That one word sends a tingle up my spine. "I want you, Jameson."

"Fuck, Shelby," I growl before taking her lips again.

I pick her up and set her on my lap so she's straddling me. She's still in the black dress, and it bunches up around her thighs as her legs part to settle on either side of mine.

Shelby winds her arms around my neck, rocking her hips against me and rubbing her panty-clad pussy all over my hardness.

Fucking hell.

Her head falls back as she moans, exposing the long column of her neck.

I lean in to lick and suck on the delicate flesh, eliciting an excited tremor when I nip the sensitive skin behind her ear.

My balls are heavy, aching with the need to spill inside her. How the hell did I get lucky enough to meet this perfect woman?

I groan and still her with a hand on her hip. "Gotta stop, baby, before I embarrass myself."

She whimpers and shoots me a desperate look, biting her lip.

"Jameson—"

God, I love the way she says my name.

"—I need you inside me."

My cock twitches. "I know, baby. I've got you. I'm going to take care of you."

I lean in and taste her lips again, allowing my hands to move over her supple body. She arches into me, purring with satisfaction at each graze of my fingertips over her skin.

I pull her dress up over her head, baring her naked breasts to my hungry gaze. Rosy pink tips pucker, begging to be licked. I happily oblige, bending to suck one into my mouth as I swirl my tongue sensuously over it.

Shelby moans, riding my hardness through my pants as if she can't help herself. I hiss a breath as her wetness seeps through her panties and my pants. My mouth salivates. I can't wait any longer to taste what's mine.

I raise my head from her nipple as she works the buttons free on my shirt. I save us both the trouble and rip the damned thing over my head. Shelby leans in and presses her lips to my chest in a sweet kiss and a lump lodges in my throat.

Lifting her, I carry her to the bed and guide her down how I want her. Her eyes never leave mine as I shuck off the rest of my clothes and my swollen cock bobs free.

Her eyes darken with lust and something more as she licks her lips, taking me in. Our first time together was in a dark cupboard, but now we get to enjoy each other in full.

I crawl up onto the bed and settle my head between her legs, gazing at her pink, ripe pussy. It glistens with moisture like morning dew on rose petals.

I breathe in deeply, inhaling her intoxicating scent. She trembles when I place my hands on her thighs, holding her open.

"Jameson—" she breathes my name and then jerks under my hands when I lick her. "Oh my god," she breathes, her thighs twitching as I lick her again, paying special attention to her pearly clit. She strains beneath me, her muscles tight as I hold her down.

"Relax, baby," I breathe, and she shivers as my breath fans across her sensitive flesh.

My cock strains, begging for attention, but I ignore it for now.

I want to taste her orgasm on my tongue.

I continue to lick her in sure strokes, delighting in her little mewls and moans. She gasps when I finally suction onto her little nub and press a finger inside her. She grips my hair and she babbles incoherently.

"Come on, baby. Give me what we both want," I encourage, knowing what she needs.

I suck hard on her little bundle of nerves, driving my finger in and out of her tight sheath.

Her strangled cry is music to my ears, better than any song I could've written. Her thighs shake as her muscles quake around my finger and her sweet juices flood my tongue.

She goes limp, and I can't wait any longer. I gather her into my arms and line myself up at her opening.

"Look at me, Shelby. I want to see those gorgeous eyes as I slide inside you."

Her eyes snap open. I sink inside her on one, heated glide.

"Fuck, you're gripping my cock like a vise," I grit, every muscle in my body tight as I fight the urge to come.

Being buried deep as I look into her eyes is enough to make me come, but I grit my teeth and hold still. One pump of my hips, and I'll spill. Hard.

I don't want that. Not yet. I want to savor this connection with her. I want to give her pleasure and feel her come all over my dick.

My chest heaves like I've run a marathon and sweat breaks out on my brow. I lean down and kiss her, loving how she arches into me, rubbing her nipples against my chest.

"Fuck, baby, I could kiss you all day, but I need to give you what you need."

"Give me everything, Jameson," she pleads, clutching at me. "I want it all."

Hearing those words is my undoing. Without further warning, I rear back and thrust hard.

Jesus, I think I've died and gone to Heaven. Her inner walls suck at me, hot, wet, and pulsing.

Shelby mewls and wraps her arms around my neck, clinging to me.

"Yes, baby. Hold on to me. I've got you," I breathe into her ear as I pull out and push in again.

We groan in unison as her pussy around me.

"More, Jameson," she pleads. "I need more."

"Goddamn, woman." I clench my teeth, pulling out and thrusting in again, hitting her deeper with each snap of my hips.

"Jameson," she purrs.

I look between our bodies as I piston in and out of her welcoming body. Licking my thumb, I rub tight circles over her clit.

"Oh god!" she moans.

I pump my hips harder. She's right on the precipice, and I'm about to push her over.

"Come with me, Shelby. Give me that pussy."

She comes with a cry of my name, her back arching up off the bed, her pussy fluttering around me.

It's too much. I join her with a hoarse shout, my balls squeezing as I spill inside her in a glorious release. I pump my hips again, emptying inside her as my orgasm tightens every muscle in my body. My entire body tingles, and I'm surprised I don't pass the fuck out.

Finally, I slump over her soft body, barely catching myself on my elbows before I crush her.

I stay buried deep inside her, loving how her pussy continues to ripple around me in little aftershocks.

Falling to my side, I draw her close, kissing her swollen lips and stroking my hands along her back. I clean her up with the utmost care and cradle her like she's precious.

And, God help me, she is. To me.

My fierce, stubborn Shelby.

The deal we made seems like it was a lifetime ago when I was a different person. I understand Shelby's concerns about dating me, but I want to grab her, run away, and leave fame and touring behind.

Shelby is practical and dedicated—she would never abandon her responsibilities. But I don't want to hide our love in the shadows.

I want to tell the world she belongs to me, but it isn't that simple. How can I convince her that the future is ours?

Chapter 11
Shelby

My stomach churns a warning, and I bolt upright in the unfamiliar hotel bed.

"Ugh, not again," I groan, throwing off the duvet that suddenly feels like it weighs a ton. I race to the bathroom, my knees hit the floor hard, and I'm bent over the porcelain bowl before I can think about being grossed out by the idea.

Just a stomach bug, I tell myself. I rinse the sour taste from my mouth and splash cool water on my face, avoiding my reflection in the mirror.

I make my way on unsteady legs back to bed, flopping onto the scratchy sheets, with the blurry impressionist print hanging crooked above the bed.

A new city every few days, living out of a suitcase, never settling in one place. I chose this lifestyle, so why am I struggling now?

My cell rings, lighting up with my sister's goofy contact pic. Her bubbly voice lifts my spirits instantly. "Happy hump day! How's life on the road?"

"Oh, you know," I reply, wedging the phone between my ear and shoulder. "Another city, another show."

Ireland laughs. "Look at you living the glam life!"

I snort. "Chaotic, not glamorous."

"You love it, you control freak." I hear a slurp as Ireland sips her coffee. "So, tell me all the juicy gossip. Any hot hookups on the crew I should know about?"

I sigh. "What happens on tour stays on tour."

"You're no fun." She sighs theatrically. "Well, at least tell me how dreamy Jameson is up close. Have you fallen madly in love yet?"

"You know it isn't like that between us."

"You said it's a publicity thing, but I've seen you two on social media, and the look in your eyes says something different." The joking tone in Ireland's voice is gone. "Whatever is going on with you two, I only want you to be happy."

"I am," I say with as much conviction as I can muster. "This job is an amazing opportunity for me. For Jameson too."

She doesn't sound convinced but lets it slide. "Are you excited for my visit? I can't wait to see you. I'm planning a spa day, obviously. Mani-pedis, massages, the works!"

The mention of massages with smelly oils and scented candles makes my stomach churn. I swallow hard. "That sounds nice," I say weakly.

"What's wrong? You sound terrible."

"Stomach bug—it's doing the rounds, playing tag with the crew. I'm the latest 'it,' apparently."

"Hey, random question about this stomach bug–but when was your last monthly visitor?"

"What?" I ask, thrown.

"You know what I mean. When did you get your last period?"

I touch my stomach absently as my mind races to do the math. The night of the concert, my friends were all there with me in the front row.

When we went back to Jameson's place, one of the times we had sex the condom broke. I believed I was in the safer phase of my cycle, but it's possible I was mistaken.

"Maybe six weeks ago?"

"Uh-oh. Are you pregnant?"

"That's impossible, I'm not–" But my protest dies on my lips.

Ireland makes a sound like she doesn't believe me. "You're catching feelings," she adds before I can argue.

My thoughts race, skidding like a car on black ice. Catching feelings? More like being bulldozed by them. And now Ireland, with her knack for seeing right through me, is calling it as she sees it.

"And what if I am? What do I do with these feelings?"

"Be brave. Embrace them," comes her swift reply.

"Listen, Shelbs," she replies. "You're in a unique situation. You have to spend a lot of time with this guy, pretend to be his girlfriend... It's only natural that you'd develop feelings for him."

Her words echo in my mind, making a surprising amount of sense. But they don't quell the storm of doubt and guilt swirling inside me.

"But it's all a lie, Ireland. A big, fat lie to the world. And what about when this is all over? He goes back to being Jameson Munroe—pop star, and I go back to being Shelby Fitzgerald."

"Then you cross that bridge when you get there," she advises. "For now, focus on the present and be honest with yourself about your feelings."

Honesty. It's such a simple concept yet feels so complicated right now.

"I'll try," I promise her.

"And remember," she adds before signing off, "sometimes life throws us curveballs to lead us where we're meant to be."

Life is throwing enough curve balls to turn me into one of those laughing clowns at the county fair. I chat with Ireland for a little while longer, but I end the call to start getting ready for work.

My mind is racing, turning over different options until a gentle knock on the door pulls me from my thoughts.

"Ready to go?" Jameson asks, offering me his hand.

"Of course," I reply with an air of confidence I don't feel.

I follow Jameson out to the waiting car, my heels clicking sharply on the pavement. My mind is spinning faster than the passing scenery as we drive to the radio station.

Pregnant. The word feels foreign and terrifying. I want to have kids one day, but am I ready to be a mother? I don't know the first thing about raising a child.

Absent-mindedly, my hand drifts to my stomach. There it is, a seed of doubt burrowing deep. I pull up the calendar on my phone, flicking back through the weeks.

My eyes narrow as I count the days, then count again. A lump forms in my throat, not from nausea this time, but the weight of what-ifs.

Jameson glances over, noticing my distress. "You okay?"

I force a tight smile. "I'm fine."

THE STUDIO'S GLASS WALLS ENCASE THE BAND like a fishbowl, their laughter and banter muted. I'm perched on a faux-leather couch, pretending to be engrossed in a magazine article about the ten best ways to wear denim—I mean, who knew there were so many?

Jameson is all charm and charisma, fielding questions with the kind of ease that suggests he was born doing interviews. His bandmates are equally adept, their laughter punctuating the room. Born entertainers, all of them.

When the radio announcer sees me peering in, he motions for me to join them. All eyes turn to me expectantly. Jameson shoots me a reassuring grin. I slide into the empty chair next to him, heat creeping up my neck as his knee brushes mine.

The reporter, a guy with more gel in his hair than I've used in my entire life, turns his attention to me.

"Touring can be tough," he says, and I brace myself. "Give us the inside scoop on these guys."

"They're dedicated professionals, which makes my job a lot easier."

The announcer presses for something interesting—gossip regarding mishaps on the road or out of control fans. The room spins, and I lose focus. A sip of water does nothing to quell the nausea.

Jameson reaches for my hand under the table and gives it a squeeze. "Everything okay?"

I offer him a tight smile that doesn't reach my eyes.

The announcer grins at me before moving on to another topic. "Jameson," he says with an air of nonchalance, "how has having Shelby on tour changed things for you personally?"

All eyes shift to Jameson, but I can feel their peripheral attention fixed on me. My stomach rebels. Clutching my abdomen discreetly under the table, I weigh my options—stay or bolt.

Jameson's hand finds mine under the table. His response is diplomatic, skirting around anything too personal. "Working with Shelby on this tour is a blessing. It's great having someone so dedicated and invested in our—"

"I'm sorry," I say before pushing back from the table abruptly.

Thankfully, the bathroom is close and I make it in time.

Leaning against the cool tile, I gulp down breaths, willing my stomach to settle. I smooth my hair, wiping my mouth with a paper towel.

As I exit the bathroom, Jameson is leaning against the wall, arms folded like a guardian angel in ripped jeans.

His dark eyes study me with concern. "You good?"

"It's nothing. Just a little stomach bug," I say quickly, tucking a strand of hair behind my ear.

"You're all shades of white," he says, his voice firm but threaded with worry. "And this is the fourth time this week. It's not 'nothing.'"

"I'm fine," I protest, crossing my arms as if that could shield me from his scrutiny.

But Jameson isn't having any of it. "Come on, we're going to see a doctor."

His arm slides under my shoulders, solid and reassuring, leaving no room for argument. He practically carries me out to the car, his arm wrapped securely around my waist.

I don't protest as I sink into the plush leather seat, the world spinning around me.

"Just breathe, Shelby. We'll get you checked out," Jameson says, sliding in beside me and nodding to the driver.

As we pull away from the radio station, I close my eyes and try to calm my churning stomach. I know Jameson's right—something isn't right here. But a tiny part of me clings to the futile hope that maybe, just maybe, it's nothing more than a persistent bug. Even as my heart knows the truth.

At the doctor's office, Jameson does all the talking, explaining my symptoms as I sit mute and numb beside him. The nurse ushers me back to an exam room alone and runs through the standard questions in a cheerful voice that grates on my frazzled nerves.

When the doctor steps in, she offers me a kind smile. Beside me, Jameson is tense, his arm brushing mine.

"We've ruled out a stomach flu, but the pregnancy test is positive. Congratulations, you're pregnant."

Although I'm sitting in a chair, the room tilts. Jameson steadies me, his voice is a low rumble, grounding me. "Easy. Breathe."

I take a deep, shuddering breath. Pregnant. The word echoes through my mind, foreign and strange and terrifying and thrilling all at once.

We listen as the doctor outlines next steps, but the words wash over me. All I can think is there's a baby growing inside me. Our baby.

Jameson helps me walk to the car, keeping an arm around my shoulders. In the quiet of the drive, tears slip down my cheeks. He reaches over, squeezing my hand.

We pull up outside the hotel. As I reach for the door, Jameson's hand on my arm stills me. I turn to face him. His eyes are soft, searching.

"Are you scared?" he asks quietly.

I consider lying, but there's no point. He can see right through me.

"Terrified," I admit. "But also happy. Is that crazy?"

A slow smile spreads across his face, softening his features. He brushes a strand of hair from my face, tucking it behind my ear.

"I'm scared too. But I'm here for you, whatever happens. You know that, right?"

Jameson reaches for my hand, his thumb grazing my knuckles.

"I promise I'll be there for you and our child. Don't stress about money. I won't walk away from this."

"Thank you," I whisper.

Jameson's rock star wealth means money won't be an issue in raising this child. That's one less thing for me to worry about at least.

Although I can't expect Jameson to love me, I know Jameson will do right by me and our baby.

My life is about to change forever. I knew there were risks, but I never imagined this outcome.

Chapter 12
Jameson

THE LIMOUSINE GLIDES to a stop at the entrance of The Music Awards. Shelby and I are about to make our official debut as a couple on the most public stage imaginable—the red carpet.

The limo driver swings the door open. I exit first and offer Shelby my arm, which she gratefully accepts. As we start down the red carpet, the camera flashes are almost blinding. Shelby's hand tightens on my arm, her nails digging in.

"You good?" I murmur, glancing at her.

Her smile is plastered on, eyes wide. "Yes, of course."

"Breathe," I say softly. "I've got you."

The farther we walk, the more frenzied the photographers become. They yell instructions, demanding different poses.

We've practiced this move more than my dance routines—the smile-and-wave, the look-of-love. But it's one thing to rehearse, another to be drowning in a sea of attention.

Shelby's tension is transmitted through her death grip on my arm.

"Jameson, look here! Shelby, over here!" The shouts come from all directions.

I wrap my arm around Shelby's waist and tuck her close to my side. Shelby nods, exhaling slowly. We pause for the photographers, turning this way and that.

"Smile for the cameras, gorgeous," I whisper, leaning close enough that my lips brush her ear.

The photographers eat it up, the camera shutters working overtime. Shelby blinks rapidly under the glare. The spotlights shine hot on my face, and I angle my body to shield her from the lights and people.

"Turn this way!" one photographer shouts.

I shift our bodies in that direction, squeezing Shelby's waist in a subtle signal to follow my lead.

We navigate the red carpet like pros, pausing to pose —a tilt of her head against my chest, my arm snug around her waist. It feels natural, and like I want to keep it there forever.

"Doing great," I murmur, keeping it light, but damn if I'm not feeling protective.

"Thanks for having my back," she says, her voice threaded with a laugh.

"Always," I reply, meaning every word.

Our eyes meet for a split second before another camera demands our attention.

"Big smiles, lovebirds!" The request sets off another round of rapid-fire shutter clicks.

"Let's give 'em a show," I say with a grin, dipping her slightly for effect.

The crowd eats it up, and Shelby lets out a laugh that's a perfect mix of nerves and excitement.

"You're a natural," I tell her, my voice low.

"Jameson Munroe, always the performer," she teases.

As we approach, reporters hold out microphones and shout questions. Shelby and I practiced for this event, but doing it for real is a big test.

"Jameson! Tell us about your new relationship status!" one woman shouts.

I angle us toward her microphone. "Shelby is an incredible woman. I'm so lucky to have her by my side," I respond smoothly, giving Shelby's waist another supportive squeeze.

Shelby stumbles over a question about our first date. The urge to protect her hits me. I wrap my arm around her waist and jump in with the fictitious details we invented.

Shelby is growing overwhelmed as more reporters clamor for our attention. She leans into me. I tighten my arm around her waist, steadying her. "Pretend it's just the two of us," I whisper.

We field a few more questions, sticking close to our rehearsed answers. The reporter eats up our act, joking about Shelby tying me down. We laugh it off convincingly. Crisis averted.

"Shelby! Shelby!"

The fans start chanting Shelby's name, not in a "hey-look-a-celebrity" way. There's genuine affection in their voices. They're tagging Shelby on social media as the girl next door who made it big.

"Oh my gosh, Shelby! We love you!" one fan gushes.

The girls cluster around Shelby, eyes shining with adoration. The fans pour praise, telling Shelby how down-to-earth and genuine she is, how she's an inspiration.

Instead of bolting, Shelby leans and greets each person warmly, asking their names and handling selfies and autographs with the ease of a seasoned pro.

Her smile comes easily, and she chats with them like they're old friends grabbing coffee.

I've witnessed her professionalism from the start, but there's more to Shelby–the lady is legit amazing. Not because she can hold down a public appearance like it's nothing, but because she cares about the people around her.

There's no pretense. It's Shelby being Shelby—warm, genuine, the kind of person who remembers your cat's name after meeting you once.

"You're so sweet, thank you," Shelby says, squeezing a girl's hand. "It was so nice meeting you all."

I squeeze in next to her. "Ready to head inside and be the perfect couple?"

Her eyes snap to mine. I see a flicker of something new—gratitude? Trust? It could be my imagination running wild. But for my part? There's nowhere else I'd rather be.

We bypass the remaining reporters and enter the awards venue. The heavy doors swing shut, muting the fandemonium outside. Away from the spotlights and shouting, Shelby's posture finally relaxes.

"That was intense," she says shakily.

It's a lot to take in for a first-timer. "You handled your fans like a seasoned pro. I'm impressed."

"I'm merely an associate celebrity—someone who associates with them," Shelby responds with a warm laugh that reverberates through my chest like a clear bell.

"The girls were sweet, and honestly, we're not so different from each other. It's only fair for me to be friendly."

Shelby glances up at me, her eyes soft. There's a glow about her, and it's not just the camera flashes or the glitz of the event. It's her—this incredible woman who's knocked me sideways with her mix of smarts and heart.

How did I get so lucky? Maybe this baby—our baby—is the start of something new. A new chapter where we can finally be honest with ourselves and each other.

There are loose ends to tie up before I come clean with my feelings.

Music will always be my first love, but what if my music career stalls? I need to prove I can offer Shelby and our baby stability and security.

I'm meeting with a big-shot Hollywood director tonight to discuss a potential acting role. This could be my ticket to finally breaking into the film industry.

This movie role could be my ticket to showing Shelby I'm husband and father material. Although I never expected to be in this position, I am, and I want to step up.

Fern Fraser

Shelby

I'm a fish out of water among the glitterati. This is Jameson's scene, not mine. My people are the ones calling for autographs from the other side of the barricades.

Yet with Jameson's hand resting on my back, I somehow fit right in. We make the perfect couple—me in a slinky dress and Jameson in a tux instead of the leather jacket he practically lives in.

We weave through the crowd toward the dance floor. The bass thumps through the soles of my feet. Around us, celebrities and industry bigwigs laugh and grind to the pulsing music. But I only have eyes for Jameson, his strong arm around my waist, his husky laugh in my ear.

"You look incredible. That dress should be illegal."

I blush, smoothing the sleek fabric over my hips. "You don't look so bad yourself, Mr. Munroe."

"Thank you, darling." Jameson winks. "Ready to dazzle 'em?"

"Born ready," I quip.

Jameson's hands rest on my hips, moving like we've been together forever instead of only a few months. It's all for show, this choreographed dance we're doing, but damn if it doesn't send a thrill up my spine.

Mid-twirl, Jameson catches a glimpse of someone over my shoulder. It's hot-shot Hollywood director Luca Regis. Jameson releases me, giving me a quick peck on the cheek before excusing himself. "Duty calls."

"Go get 'em, tiger."

Waiters circulate hors d'oeuvres and a waiter appears with champagne. I decline, citing a sensitive stomach and choose soda instead.

Jameson is engaged in a serious discussion with a renowned director from Hollywood. This could be his chance to break into the highly competitive film industry.

Our fake romance is serving its purpose. He's getting the opportunities he deserves.

As for me, I'm trying hard not to spill the drink all over my dress.

Jameson glances my way, blowing a discreet kiss. I smile through the bittersweet ache in my chest. Jameson needs me to be his steady anchor.

We had a deal—no strings attached. And a baby seems like a pretty big "string."

It's incredibly hot, and the crowded atmosphere is messing with my senses.

"Shelby, right? I'm Marcus." A smooth voice interrupts my people-watching. "I've heard great things about your work on the Soul Obsession tour."

"Thank you," I reply, turning toward the newcomer and shaking his hand. Firm grip, salt-and-pepper hair, and tailored suit. Yep, total exec.

"You clearly know how to handle these rockstar types."

I laugh. "Oh, I don't know about that."

Marcus gestures around the room. "There are some important people here tonight. I'd love to introduce you if you have time later."

This opportunity was what I'd been hoping for in my career. "Thank you, I'd appreciate that."

Marcus' eyes flick down my body appreciatively. "Maybe afterward, we could continue the conversation. Over dinner, perhaps?"

Ah. There's the catch.

I force a smile, ignoring the way my stomach twists. "That's flattering, but I'm here with someone." I nod toward Jameson.

"A woman like you with Jameson Munroe?" Marcus scoffs, and there's an edge to his tone. "You deserve better. Don't let yourself get played."

I stiffen, meeting his gaze directly. "Reputation or not, I'm quite content."

We're interrupted by a server. Turning sharply on my heel, I melt into the crowd. The cold night air is like a shock to my system after the stuffy heat of the auditorium.

"What a creep," I mutter myself, taking deep breaths as I lean against the cold metal railing.

I grow tired of waiting and don't wish to run into Marcus. Hopefully, Jameson's finished talking to Luca and has good news to share.

I take a deep breath and push through the heavy double doors into the crowded auditorium. The noise hits me like a wave—laughter, clinking glasses, overlapping conversations. I blink under the glaring lights, scanning the room for Jameson.

Instead, I spot the record exec making a beeline toward me. Great.

"We never got to finish our little chat earlier." His breath reeks of scotch, and his tie is askew. "Come on, one drink. Loosen up a little."

Nausea roils in my stomach. "I'm all good, thanks." I try to sidestep him, but he grabs my wrist, his grip surprisingly strong.

A shiver of discomfort wriggles its way up my spine. The noise of the party fades, everything narrowing down to this unwelcome contact.

My mind races, searching for an exit strategy that doesn't involve violence or vomit.

I search the sea of faces for those familiar brooding eyes. But I don't see Jameson. It's just me and Handsy McGrabby here.

Fantastic.

"Let go of me," I say through gritted teeth.

When I try to tug my arm free, his grip tightens.

"Get your hands off her," Jameson growls, prying the exec's fingers off me.

The exec stumbles. "Stay out of this, pretty boy. A real man's talking to the lady here."

"She's with me," Jameson announces, loud enough for surrounding conversations to pause and heads to turn. His jaw looks like it's been chiseled out of stone. "Back off."

The exec laughs. "Or what? Gonna mess up that pretty face of yours?"

Jameson's eyes blaze, his jaw clenched. "You've got three seconds to get out of here before I knock out your teeth."

The murmur of conversation has dialed down to a hush as necks crane and eyes peek over champagne flutes, hungry for some A-list drama.

"Jameson, it's fine." I grab his arm. "Let's go."

Jameson shields me with his body, glaring daggers at the exec. "Apologize. Now."

The exec snorts. "Make me, punk."

My rescuer stands toe-to-toe with the exec, close enough that I can see the muscle twitching in his cheek. Jameson's hand clenches into a fist at his side. My heart races.

"Jameson, stop," I plead, unsure how to proceed when Rick appears, pulling Jameson aside.

"Walk away. Now," Rick orders under his breath. "You're gonna blow your career sky-high if you deck this guy."

Jameson turns to me, eyes refocusing like he's snapping out of a daydream. The fire in his eyes softens. "Are you okay?"

I nod, rubbing my wrist. "I'm fine."

Jameson gently takes my hand, turning my wrist to examine the red marks. "I'm sorry. I shouldn't have lost my cool."

I shoot him a sly grin. "Thanks for coming to the rescue, but I had the situation under control."

"Of course, but I regret leaving you to go and talk to Luca." He runs a hand through his hair in frustration.

"Seeing that creep with his hands on you made me feel–"

His eyes search mine, vulnerable and full of longing. "I'll always protect you, both of you," he adds softly, his gaze dropping to our child growing inside me.

My heart fills with love as Jameson's gaze drops to my mouth. He brushes a stray hair from my face, his fingers warm against my skin. "I love you. I don't want to pretend anymore. I want this—want us— for real."

"Me too."

Without hesitation, I lean in and press my lips against his, pouring all of my love and relief into the kiss. We break apart, foreheads touching.

"What happened in your meeting with Luca? Am I looking at Hollywood's new rising star?" I ask in an excited rush.

"He offered me a role in his new film." My heart leaps for joy, but Jameson pauses, signaling a caveat. "It was a great opportunity, and I was honored, but I turned it down."

Confusion furrows my brow. "Why? Did you change your mind about acting?"

He looks at me with such intensity, his resolve clear. "Filming starts when our baby is due. I'm not missing the birth of our child."

My vision blurs. "Jameson. I don't know what to say."

His hand settles gently over my swelling belly, protective and loving. "My perspective changed since you came into my life. You and our baby are my priority now."

I throw my arms around him. "You have no idea how much that means to me," I whisper against his chest, my voice muffled by his warmth.

I finally step back, wiping away a tear. "Where does this leave your music career? Is your solo album still due for release?"

He nods confidently. "The album is on schedule for release. Music will always be part of my life. But I want to watch our baby grow up, not miss out because I'm off touring or promoting an album. The fame and success—it'll mean nothing if I'm not there for the moments that matter."

"I've never tried sharing my life with anyone before, never even come close to marriage," he says. "This is new to me."

I look at him with tears in my eyes, overwhelmed by his words. I place my hand on my belly protectively. "It's all new for me too."

I never thought I could have it all—a loving partner and a child on the way. It's more than I ever dreamed of.

"Who needs a fancy condo?" I mumble to myself.

"What condo?"

Epilogue
Jameson

THE RELATIONSHIPS from my past seem inconsequential now, shadows compared to the sun that is Shelby. "I love you. I'll be good to you and faithful. I'll give you everything you need."

The vow feels sacred, a covenant between her heart and mine.

Shelby smiles and pulls me in for a soft, lingering kiss. As we hold each other close, I know, without a doubt, I'm kissing my future wife, the mother of my child. But I need to make it official.

Suddenly, Rick appears, grinning from ear to ear. "Fuz-E Slip-R, the rapper who accused you of stealing his lyrics? He dropped the charges. His lawyers found other artists about to sue him for plagiarizing their work. They suggested he drop the suit once they knew he was guilty."

My tense muscles relax as Rick's words sink in. "Thanks for the update." At least now I can start fresh without this hanging over my head. "Oh, and one more thing. Can you issue a press release?"

Rick pauses. "Sure, what's the announcement?"

I take a deep breath. This is it. "I know we didn't plan any of this," I say, bringing one of Shelby's hands to my lips for a kiss. "I love Shelby and want to spend my life with her."

Rick claps me on the shoulder. "I'm happy for you, man."

I grab his arm to stop him from leaving. "Wait. There's something else."

I lean in to whisper in Shelby's ear. Her eyes widen with excitement and she nods eagerly as I turn back to Rick.

"Shelby's carrying our child," I declare, watching his reaction.

Rick's jaw drops in disbelief. "Congratulations, you two!" he says with a smile. "I'll let you get back to your evening."

Shelby's eyes glisten. "I'm so proud of you," she whispers, her voice thick with emotion.

As I gaze into her shining eyes, I know I've made the right choice. "I love you."

Shelby smiles radiantly and kisses me again. "I love you too. And I can't wait to tell everyone the news!"

"Before we spread the news, there's something I want to do first." My self-control dissolves, and I pull her closer, my need for her growing with every passing second. "You're all I want. Right here, right now."

"Jameson Munroe, you are insane," she accuses, but her protest dissolves into a deep husky laugh.

"Absolutely." I pull her close, hand splayed on the small of her back, feeling the heat through the silk of her dress. We make a beeline to the closest dressing room marked 'Private.'

"Breaking rules now, are we?" She's trying to be stern, but her eyes twinkle.

"Only the boring ones."

The lock clicks shut, and suddenly, we're cocooned in this tiny dressing room, the noise of the party fading away. Her cheeks are flushed, eyes bright.

She's so beautiful it makes my chest ache. Her full lips curve in a soft invitation that has my insides doing somersaults.

"Well, Munroe, I hope you have a plan here," she says, lips quirking.

I step closer, backing her against the door. "Oh, I've got a plan, baby. You're all I think about. Day, night— it's always you." I brush my fingers down her bare arm, and she shivers. "I'm gonna kiss every inch of you until you're begging for more."

Her breath hitches as I lean in, nuzzling her neck. She smells incredible, like vanilla and jasmine —a scent that will forever be etched into my memory as hers.

"Goodness gracious, Munroe, it's a little risky, don't you think?" Her voice is threaded with excitement, not disapproval. She's on board for this crazy ride.

I growl, feeling like some prehistoric man claiming his mate. "If we're going to do everything in the public eye, we may as well go all the way."

Shelby unbuttons my shirt, trailing kisses down my chest and abs. I shudder with pleasure, running my hands through her silky hair. "You're driving me crazy."

She looks up at me, eyes dark with desire. With a wicked grin, Shelby purrs, "I'm in charge now, rockstar."

"Yes, ma'am." This incredible woman owns me, heart and soul.

Every nerve ending sizzles with anticipation. I'm so ready to let her take control. As she eagerly takes me into her mouth, struggling to fit all of me, I grunt in satisfaction.

Shelby's plump lips are wrapped around me, her skilled tongue gliding up and down my shaft.

She may look small and fragile, but there's nothing tame about this wild woman devouring me fervently.

I'm at her mercy, with my head thrown back and my body tensing under her touch. She has me by the balls, literally.

She holds all the power, controlling every sensation as she sucks me in and out of her mouth. I'm under her spell, and I never want it to end.

"Fuck, baby." I wrap her hair around my fist. "Your mouth feels so good."

I start moving my hips back and forth, feeling her gag as she struggles to take me. Tears are streaming down her face, but she bravely continues to pleasure me as I thrust deeper and faster.

"Swallow every last drop when I cum," I growl, my body stilling as I cup her face.

With a groan, my head dips back as I release into her mouth. She swallows it all, moaning her pleasure and making me shudder.

Pulling her to her feet, I slide her thong aside and tease her delicate folds, mesmerized by the sight of her pussy. I want to taste her, feel her cum on my tongue.

My mouth waters at the thought. She's writhing as I play with her pussy. The sounds she's making drive me wild—I can't get enough.

It's only been a hot minute since I came down her throat but I'm already hard again. Dropping to my knees, I dip down and devour her.

"Jameson," she cries out, clutching my shoulders. Shelby's orgasm is instant—she's screaming but I don't stop sucking her clit.

"God, look at us," Shelby breathes, her gaze locked on our reflections. There's something wickedly voyeuristic about watching ourselves, a feedback loop of desire that cranks the heat to inferno levels.

"Best show in town," I say, though my voice is more husky than witty. My hands roam over her, hungry for the feel of her skin, while our mirrored selves put on one hell of a performance.

She arches an eyebrow, all sultry confidence and heart-stopping smile, even as her fingers tangle in my hair, pulling me closer. "Encore?"

Necessary clothing unzipped or pushed aside, I can't wait any longer. "Only if you promise to scream my name."

"Always. I'm your number one fan."

I reach down, guiding myself to her entrance. We both moan as I push inside. She feels fantastic, hot and tight around me.

We move together, finding our rhythm. With each thrust, we climb higher, pleasure coiling tight. Her moans spur me on. I want to make her come undone. I shift angles, and she shudders, nails digging into my skin.

"Oh god, right there," she gasps.

I increase my pace, hitting that sweet spot over and over. Her moans get louder, and I feel her tightening around me. "Come for me, baby," I rasp in her ear.

She shatters with a wordless cry, pulsing around me. The sensation sends me over the edge right after her. We collapse in a sweaty, sated heap, struggling to catch our breath.

"That was—" Shelby pants.

"Incredible," I finish, kissing her tenderly.

Epilogue 2
Shelby

8 Years Later

TONIGHT IS the premiere of Jameson's gritty and highly-anticipated crime drama, "Under the Neon Sky," a project he hopes will establish his reputation as a serious actor.

I'm standing in front of the full-length mirror in our bedroom, adding the finishing touches to my outfit. The deep burgundy silk dress skims over my hips before cascading to the floor in layers.

I smooth out non-existent wrinkles more from habit than necessity. Even after all these years, the glitz and glamour of a red carpet premiere makes me a little nervous.

From this vantage, I have a clear view into the nursery where Jameson is rocking our infant son, Liam. Jameson is singing softly, an upbeat lullaby that reminds me of the pop tunes that catapulted him to fame.

Jameson is tracing a finger down Liam's plump cheek. My husband's eyes are filled with that unquenchable love I recognize from our early days of being in love. Only now, he shares that love with our children— Isabella, 7, and baby Liam.

When our eyes meet, we exchange a loving glance. Our connection is deeper than ever, and I remember how far we've come. Jameson kept his promises when we first went public with the news we were a couple.

Following Isabella's birth, Jameson stepped back from touring to be a more present husband and father.

Through an adjacent room, our daughter Isabella, a curious and lively girl, is practicing piano, trying to mimic the melody her father is singing to Liam. She has Jameson's passion and creativity, always making up songs and playing pretend. Seeing her follow in Jameson's artistic footsteps makes my heart swell.

This cocky celebrity rebel softened into a dedicated father and husband, choosing love over fame. These days, he is producing music for other artists while occasionally releasing his own material.

When Jameson tried transitioning to acting, he faced skepticism from critics who said he was another pop star trying to crossover. I believed in his talent and had no doubt he would succeed. Jameson can do anything he puts his mind to. Jameson took it as a personal challenge, throwing himself into intense acting workshops and auditions. I'll never forget the unbridled joy on his face when he landed his first major role.

Jameson saunters into the bedroom, adjusting his tie. "You look incredible," he says, eyes sweeping over me appreciatively.

"And you're going to be late for your premiere, Mr. Movie Star," I chide playfully.

He looks devastatingly handsome in a tailored suit. Although at almost 40, he has a few more lines etched into his handsome face, his eyes still sparkle. And his artfully tousled hair hints at the rebellious edge he loves to flaunt so proudly.

Jameson's gaze softens. "None of this would be happening without you," he says earnestly. "You kept us steady when everything was stormy."

Cupping his cheek, I say with quiet pride, "Look at us now—you're finding success on the big screen, and my event planning company is booming. Isabella's following in your artistic footsteps and Liam's cute laughter makes our home complete. We made it work."

A beat passes, filled with the weight and warmth of our shared memories. So much has changed since the chaos of that music tour brought us together. Back then, I never imagined we'd end up here—happily married with two beautiful children, careers we love, and a home filled with creativity and laughter.

It wasn't always easy. The media scrutiny was intense, even after the initial stunt ended. But we weathered it together. When Jameson decided to leave the band, speculation ran rampant. I encouraged him to follow his passion. The public didn't know that tender, artistic soul like I did.

There were challenges balancing family and careers, but we compromised. Seeing Jameson glow with pride and purpose, I know it was all worth it. We built something real, beyond the limelight and labels.

Jameson glances at his watch. "We should get going," he says. But he pulls me in for a lingering kiss first. When we break apart, foreheads touching, his voice is a rough whisper. "I love you, Shelby Munroe. Always."

My heart flutters, just like that first fake date so long ago. "I love you too," I murmur.

"Well then, what are we waiting for? Let's show them who we are."

Laughing, I take his proffered arm. We descend the stairs together, where our daughter is with the babysitter, waiting eagerly by the door. Isabella's dark hair is swept back with a glittery barrette, and her sweet face glows with excitement for her daddy. She slips her tiny hand into mine.

"Ready, my darlings?" Jameson asks. We nod in unison.

In the darkened theater, Jameson sinks into his seat beside me, leg jiggling nervously. I squeeze his hand and lean in close as the opening credits begin.

"Eyes forward, Mr. Leading Man. Your adoring public awaits."

Jameson relaxes a bit and wraps an arm around me. I nestle against his shoulder, beyond proud to be here supporting the man I love. The film is even better than I'd hoped. Jameson ignites the screen with a raw, compelling performance that leaves me awestruck.

When the credits roll, the theater erupts into thunderous applause. I join in vigorously, turning to Jameson with shining eyes. "You were amazing! I'm so proud of you."

He turns to me, his brown eyes catching mine with that same intensity that drew me in all those years ago. "Only because I have you by my side," he replies softly before pressing a kiss to my forehead.

Afterward, we make our way to the exclusive after-party. I balance a sleepy Isabella on one hip while holding Jameson's hand. Cameras flash, capturing this new high point in his career—a career that has taken many turns but ultimately led him here.

When it's time for Jameson to make a speech, he stands at a podium, addressing an elegantly dressed crowd. The buzz of conversation fades as he begins to speak.

"Music has been my guiding force," Jameson starts, "but it's more than a personal journey. It's about what we can give back."

Jameson shares his passionate beliefs about the importance of music education with the crowd. He shares news of the academy we've started funding to support musicians with their aspirations—a project close to both our hearts. It's not about nurturing talent or creating more lucrative boy bands. The academy is about giving kids a chance to fulfill their dreams.

The pride in my chest blooms like a rose in full flourish—I've seen all sides of Jameson Munroe—the artist, the fighter, the lover, and now this man standing tall in front of admirers and supporters alike.

"None of this would've been possible without my partner in crime, the brains of the operation, and the most amazing person I've had the good fortune to meet—my wife, Shelby."

I feel a rush of warmth as all eyes turn to me. I'm not one for the spotlight. As I wave to the crowd, my cheeks tinge with a shade that rivals my burgundy dress. I smile up at Jameson. Balancing my career and family life has never been easy, but moments like these make every challenge worth it.

"And let's not forget our daughter Isabella. Isa, baby, stand up and say hi."

Clutching my hands for balance, Isabella pops up, giving a little twirl that makes her black curls bounce. The audience melts, clapping wildly for Jameson's mini-me.

My daughter's smile is worth more than any accolade or recognition. I hold her close as she sits down, whispering encouragement in her ear, "You did great, sweetie. And so did your daddy!"

Isabella nods excitedly. "Yeah! Everyone clapped for him."

Jameson wraps up his speech and rejoins us at the table. He squeezes my shoulder and quickly kisses Isabella's forehead before taking his seat beside us.

Jameson takes my hand under the table, his fingers entwining with mine.

"You were amazing tonight," I say softly.

"I couldn't have done any of this without you," he murmurs into my hair.

I pull back slightly to meet his gaze—those deep brown eyes that have become my world—and shake my head slightly.

"It was always 'us,' "I remind him gently. "And it always will be."

Dear Reader,

I want to thank you from the bottom of my heart, for reading **Boy Band Baby Bump**. My goal with writing is to lift your spirits and make you smile. I hope you enjoyed **Jameson and Shelby's** story.

Did you know there are other titles available with the **Galentines** theme?

Romancing the Billionaire

I'm on vacay at a writers' retreat with my besties, and

after a few too many drinks, I blurt my secret. Despite writing super-hot romance books or a living, I don't have any real-life experience. Lucky for me, the super-hot groundskeeper at the mountain resort is just the man to help me solve my 'V-card problem.'

Wild at Heart

I'm trespassing on private land, protesting to save the forest when I get stuck in a tree. A handsome stranger helps me, but a simple rescue spirals out of control when the police show up and arrest us for trespassing. By the time I realize who he is, I'm in over my head.

Fern Fraser

Subscribe to my VIP Newsletter and get a free
NSFW novella.
https://www.fernfraser.com/free-book

Fern Fraser

USA Today Bestselling Author Fern Fraser writes light-hearted, high-heat contemporary short romances.

Fern's fun, fast-paced romances feature women who know what they want. Her heroes are over-the-top alphas who instantly fall head-over-heels in love. Full of heart, suspense, action, and laughs, Fern's romances give you all the feels in half the time.

Fern Fraser: All the Feels in Half the Time.

Fern Fraser is represented by Laura Pink from the
SBR Media

You can find Fern at
https://www.fernfraser.com/

amazon.com/author/fernfraser

bookbub.com/authors/fern-fraser

facebook.com/FernFraserAuthor

instagram.com/authorfernfraser

Milton Keynes UK
Ingram Content Group UK Ltd.
UKHW012247290324
440241UK00004B/171

9 798224 672974